OTHER YEARLING BOOKS YOU WILL ENJOY:

THE POOL PARTY, *Gary Soto*
THE SKIRT, *Gary Soto*
THE BLACK PEARL, *Scott O'Dell*
ISLAND OF THE BLUE DOLPHINS, *Scott O'Dell*
ZIA, *Scott O'Dell*
THUNDER ROLLING IN THE MOUNTAINS,
Scott O'Dell and Elizabeth Hall
UNDER THE BLOOD-RED SUN, *Graham Salisbury*
NEVER TRUST A SISTER OVER 12, *Stephen Roos*
HOW TO EAT FRIED WORMS, *Thomas Rockwell*
HOW TO FIGHT A GIRL, *Thomas Rockwell*

ARLING BOOKS are designed especially to entertain and
lighten young people. Patricia Reilly Giff, consultant
this series, received her bachelor's degree from Mary-
ount College and a master's degree in history from St.
an's University. She holds a Professional Diploma
Reading and a Doctorate of Humane Letters from
ofstra University. She was a teacher and reading con-
ltant for many years, and is the author of numerous
oks for young readers.

For a complete listing of all Yearling titles, write to
Dell Readers Service,
P.O. Box 1045,
South Holland, IL 60473.

y
e
to
n
Jo
in
F
s
b

Gary Soto

Boys
at
Work

Illustrated by Robert Casilla

A Yearling Book

Published by
Bantam Doubleday Dell Books for Young Readers
a division of
Bantam Doubleday Dell Publishing Group, Inc.
1540 Broadway
New York, New York 10036

ISBN: 0-440-41221-8

Reprinted by arrangement with Delacorte Press

Printed in the United States of America

August 1996

10 9 8 7 6 5 4 3 2 1

CWO

for José Novoa

BOYS AT WORK

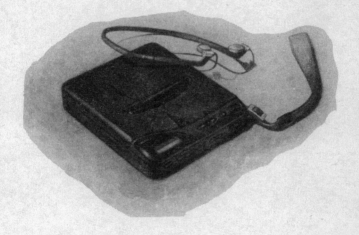

Chapter **1**

Rudy and Alex had been pals ever since they were three years old and were pulled along by bigger kids on their first trick-or-treat. Each had gone as a baby pirate, a patch over one eye, waving a stick for a sword. The boys tripped and fell over steps and hilly lawns. They cried hot tears that disappeared when they were handed sticky popcorn balls wrapped in cellophane.

Now it was summer, and they were ten years old. They sat on the front porch, scared as two cats dunked in pond water. But it wasn't water that had them shivering. They had been playing baseball with some kids from the neighborhood. Rudy had tripped while rounding third base wildly and landed, knees first, on a pile of equipment. When he rose from the ground, knees scraped, he saw among the jerseys, bats, and mitts a smashed Discman.

Danny, one of the players, pointed at the splintered Discman and then at Rudy. "My brother Slinky is gonna kill you!"

"It was an accident."

"Big deal! He's still going to kill you. I feel sorry for you."

"He said it was an accident," Alex growled in return. He puffed his chest out and tried to look tough.

"It won't be an accident when he smashes your face!" Danny spat. "You two better get out of town."

With that, Rudy and Alex ran away, legs kicking high, now and then looking over their shoulders. When Danny's older brother, Slinky, found out, he would come collect. Slinky was a *vato loco*. Already he had a tattoo cut into the web of skin between his index finger and thumb. Already he had spent a month in juvenile hall, scratching his name into the wall. He was bad, they heard. Slinky even shot BB's through the gap between his front teeth.

For the moment, they were sweating not from nerves but from the heat of the summer day. Their cooked faces were the color of dunked crabs. They drank ice water, but even that didn't help. The day was hot, and it was bound to get hotter once Slinky found out.

"It wasn't my fault," Rudy said again, kicking a stone.

"Mala suerte," Alex agreed. "They shouldn't have put their stuff there."

"Do you think Danny's brother will get us?" Rudy asked. "I heard he hits hard."

"Let's stay out of sight," Alex suggested. "Maybe we should get out of town."

"How? We can't drive. Anyways, Slinky will find us."

They jumped when the telephone rang inside Rudy's house. Rudy's sister, Estela, answered the phone and began to coo softly at her boyfriend of one whole week, some guy named Larry "Weasel" Sanchez, a homeboy from Sequoia Junior High.

"Man, I wish I was rich," Rudy lamented.

"I could buy Slinky a new Discman." Two flies circled overhead, heavy bombers with bluish bellies. "Alex, maybe I should get a job," he added as he swatted at the flies and missed.

"¡Simón!" Alex said brightly. "That's what you need—a job! You'll have the money in no time."

Rudy's face lit up. From the porch, he eyed the lawn mower leaning against the house.

"Hey, man," Alex said after he followed Rudy's gaze. "You can cut some lawns."

"You gonna help me?" Rudy asked.

"Sure, you're *mi carnal*."

"Thanks, homes."

They shook hands, raza-style.

Rudy didn't like mowing, but he didn't like the idea of Slinky rattling his head either. He had just learned division in school, and the thought of it being punched out of his head made him sick.

"Okay." Rudy sighed. "Let's give it a try." They stood up, brushing the bottoms of their jeans. While Alex got the lawn mower, Rudy hurried to the garage for a rake. Rudy found one with some of its teeth missing. Next he found a pair of stiff work gloves that his father wore when pruning the hedge. He grabbed them and returned whistling to the front yard.

"Where should we go?" Rudy asked.

"Let's try Mrs. Estrada," Alex suggested. "She's cool."

Mrs. Estrada was a woman with thirteen cats. They knew she was a soft touch because at Halloween she cackled like a witch with a broom between her legs and threw fistfuls of candy into their shopping bags. She also gave them apples that they didn't have to take down to the police station to X-ray.

"Yeah, Mrs. Estrada," Rudy said hopefully. "I bet she has some work."

They hurried up the street. As Alex pushed the lawn mower, the blades spun out gusts of warm wind. Rudy jabbed the rake like a spear, happy that he was about to earn some money. He had earned money once before, when his older cousin begged him to be the ring bearer in his wedding. Rudy didn't like the idea of walking down the aisle of his church dressed in a white tuxedo, especially in short pants. But what convinced him was the scent of money. His cousin had forked over a sweet ten-dollar bill that later went toward gobs of candy.

"She's home," Rudy said, pointing as they rounded the corner onto her street.

Mrs. Estrada was on her front porch draining her aquarium, a long lap of greenish water spilling over the porch. She looked up and smiled, both of her front teeth gone. In their place was a black space and a wiggle of a pink tongue.

"Hello, Mrs. Estrada," Rudy said as he approached her. " 'Member us?"

She looked at Rudy and Alex almost suspiciously, one eye glinting. She said, "I know your faces. You're my grandsons, ¿que no?"

Rudy gulped as he turned and widened his eyes at Alex. It had been many months since they had seen her last, and maybe she was losing her memory. On the bottom of her aquarium he noticed a layer of cat's-eye marbles. Maybe she was losing her marbles, Rudy wondered.

"No, we're boys looking for work," Rudy said. "You need your lawn cut?"

"My lawn?" she questioned. "What's wrong with my lawn?"

"You know, it's . . . long. It needs a trim, señora," Rudy said as he pounded the handle of the lawn mower.

As Mrs. Estrada turned to look at her lawn, a fish slipped from the aquarium and flopped over the edge of the porch. A herd of marbles rolled out as well. Mrs. Estrada cried, "Not again!"

"I'll help," Rudy shouted.

Crouching, Rudy searched for the fish, parting the bushes that surrounded the porch. He dropped to his knees, careful not to smash the fish as he had the Discman. Rudy gathered up the fish, its mouth opening and closing like a wound. Its tail beat frantically.

"Poor thing," Rudy said as he rose slowly to his feet.

"Looks okay to me," Alex said, peeking between the bushes. "He just got a little dirt on him." He spotted the marbles, some of them caked with dirt. He jumped into the bush and gathered them too.

Rudy climbed the front porch steps and handed the flopping fish to Mrs. Estrada, who took it into her palms and smiled her toothless smile at it. She turned her gaze to the boys and then whirled around and went inside the house. The boys followed her, almost tripping over her thirteen cats, who looked at Rudy and Alex. They had been wrestling on the rug, hanging by their claws from the curtains and ambushing each other around the corners of the sofa.

"There, there, you bad fishy," Mrs. Estrada said as she rinsed the fish, a common zebra danio. She placed it in a pan brimming with water and turned to the boys. She wrung her hands into a dish towel. "Now what is this about my lawn?"

"Well, me and Alex are looking for work."

"You are looking for work?" Mrs. Estrada repeated. "You boys want a job?"

"Yeah—anything," Rudy beamed.

"Anything?" Mrs. Estrada repeated.

"Yeah, I even have my social security number. It's five-six-three—" Alex started to blabber.

But Mrs. Estrada cut Alex off with a slice of her hand across her throat. She ushered the boys to the living room, where the thirteen cats were back at play. Two of them were playing tug-of-war with a dish towel.

"I want you to clean my cats," Mrs. Estrada instructed.

"You mean wash them?" Rudy asked, confused.

Mrs. Estrada shook her head. She left for a

moment and returned to the kitchen. The cats, all feisty and still working with nine lives apiece, jumped playfully at Rudy and Alex. When Rudy stepped back, two kittens climbed onto his shoes, meowing and clinging to his pants legs. It looked as if Rudy and the two kittens were dancing.

"How come Mrs. Estrada has so many cats?" Rudy asked as he shook his leg and the cats went tumbling. They immediately jumped at each other and began to wrestle.

"I don't know. Maybe she's lonely," Alex said as he took an orange cat into his arms. He pressed his nose to the cat's nose, but the cat hissed and swatted Alex.

Mrs. Estrada returned to the living room with two flea combs. She held them up and sang, "Here's a job for you *chamacos*!"

Rudy looked at the cats, all tumbling and fighting each other or racing around the furniture. He took a comb from Mrs. Estrada. He had imagined pushing his dad's mower over lawns, earning decent money for decent work. He had imagined that he would be bubbling with sweat and sneezing from the grass clippings. He had imagined hard, manly work. But he was wrong. His first summer job was to comb the bloody fleas from a litter of cats, all nameless and full of fury and biting play. The first cat hissed and scratched for freedom as Rudy plucked it up by the scruff of its neck.

Rudy and Alex got to work, sending the fleas and the cats to their wayward destiny.

Chapter 2

Rudy and Alex combed the thirteen struggling cats, squashing a tribe of fat fleas to death between their fingernails. They earned a dollar each and two goldfish, which Mrs. Estrada insisted they take home in styrofoam cups. They gave the goldfish to Alex's baby sister, Aurelia.

The next day, Rudy and Alex went from cats to dogs when Rudy remembered his *nina*, a retired teacher. Now they were in her backyard repairing the doghouse. Rudy pounded a nail into an asphalt shingle on the roof. He nailed and wiped his brow. The sun was fierce, a big bully hammering down on the people in their valley town.

"I guess it's done," he said to Alex, who sat in the shade scratching behind the ear of Curly, his *nina*'s mutt. Curly lay with his legs in the air. When Alex scratched in earnest, the tongue-flopping dog bicycled his legs in contentment.

Alex stood up and approached the rickety doghouse. When he patted the new roof, the house swayed under the weight of the asphalt shingles. "I think you put too many on, Rudy," he concluded.

Rudy rocked the doghouse. For a moment, Rudy imagined a hard rain collapsing the house on Curly while he slept.

"Maybe I'd better take some off," Rudy said.

They pried up the nails and peeled off a layer of shingles.

Rudy's *nina*, Mrs. Castillo, came out onto the back porch. She wore a dress printed with flowers. Her mouth was a bud of red, red lipstick. She smiled and descended the steps with two trumpet-size *chicharrones*, pork rinds.

"It could keep out a tornado," Mrs. Castillo remarked as she admired the doghouse. She handed the *chicharrones* to the boys and they took them with a soft *"gracias."*

"How was school this year?" his *nina* asked.

"It was okay. I got an A in lunch."

Rudy and Alex laughed at their old joke. His *nina* smiled with them.

"Next, I want you to clean out the garage," she instructed.

She told them to gather the newspapers and magazines and throw them in the Dumpster. She also asked them to stack the paint cans and sweep up.

"And if you see anything you want, go ahead and take it."

Mrs. Castillo paid Rudy and Alex three dollars each. She told them that she had to get ready to go shopping. After she returned inside the house, Rudy and Alex bit into their *chicharrones*. They crunched on their back molars—hard!

"Man, mine's like a hammer," Rudy joked. He pretended to hammer a nail with it. He broke off a piece and gave it to Curly. The dog took it between his paws and began to gnaw on it, growling under his breath.

Rudy heard his *nina*'s car pull out of the driveway. Curly started howling, his head tilted upward.

"*Cálmate*," Rudy said. "Chill out, Curly. She'll be back with some grub for you."

Finished with their snack, Rudy and Alex approached the garage, wiping their hands on their jeans. When they pulled open the garage door, they were surprised at their luck.

"*Mira*, look at the cans!" Rudy shouted.

"*¡Chihuahua!*" Alex exclaimed.

Rudy and Alex hovered over the five plastic trash bags brimming with aluminum soda cans. Rudy picked up a bag and hugged it. He whistled and said, "We can get some coins for this stash."

"Go for it," Alex agreed. "Your *nina* said we could have anything we want."

They lugged the bags outside and leaned them against the garage door. Then they got to work, sweeping and throwing the newspapers and magazines into the Dumpster. They stacked the paint cans into a neat pyramid. They wiped dust from the washer and dryer and swatted spiderwebs in the dark corners.

They gathered the tools spilled from the tool-box. Curly lay on the cement floor, occasionally barking out commands.

After they finished, they took a long drink from the garden hose to cool off. They washed their faces and hands. They examined their aluminum cans. They found that his *nina* preferred Pepsi to Coke.

"How we gonna carry them?" Rudy asked.

"I don't know," Alex said with a shrug. He looked around the yard and then behind the garage, where they discovered another trash bag of soda cans. "We need something like a wheelbarrow."

With Curly in tow, they returned to the garage and stood in the doorway, hands on their hips. There was no wheelbarrow, no shopping cart.

"How 'bout that?" Rudy said, pointing.

"What?"

"The door, Alex."

A door with blistering paint leaned against the wall.

"We can put our bags on it," Rudy explained. "I'll get one end and you get the other."

"I guess it'll work." Alex knocked on the

door and, his voice pitched high, said, "Who is it?" Rudy followed along. "It's me, Little Red Riding Hood, *carnal*!"

The boys laughed at their joke. They then dusted off the door, carried it outside, and laid it on the grass. They piled the six trash bags on it and tied Curly to the clothesline. For good measure, they scratched behind Curly's ear. Then, with Rudy in front and Alex in back, they counted, *"Uno, dos, tres."* With a grunt, they lifted the door, knees nearly buckling. They swayed as they tried to balance the weight of the aluminum cans.

"This feels weird," Rudy said.

"Real weird," Alex agreed.

"I guess this is how Stone Age people did it, before they invented wheels."

"Nah, homes, they used camels first, and then it was doors," Alex corrected Rudy.

"Are you sure?"

"Sure I'm sure. First camels, and then someone got smart and started using doors. I read it in a book."

Rudy shrugged his shoulders. He was glad for such a loyal and smart friend, and he told him so. "Alex, man, you got a lot of good brains inside your head. I know I can count on you."

They started up the street, the cans rattling in the bags like a treasure of silver spoons and forks. They headed in the direction of the recycling center on Belmont Avenue. At first, it was easy. But when their arms started aching, their steps became heavy as bricks. Still, Rudy and Alex kept going. They could see that they had a fortune in aluminum cans. They could see that with this one haul, the replacement Discman would become a reality.

"Let's rest," Rudy suggested after a mile. They stopped under a shade tree, fanning their hot faces. They threw themselves on the grass that grew along the curb.

"I wish I had a soda." Alex sighed.

"Me too," Rudy agreed. He patted one of the plastic bags and remarked, "Man, my *nina* drinks a lot of sodas."

"*De veras*, homes."

They lay on the grass, eyes closed and exhausted. A breeze swirled over their bodies. A mockingbird chirped in the tree with sagging leaves. Rudy was licking his dry lips and thinking about a simple glass of water brimming with ice cubes, when he heard a growling, "Hey, you punks! *¡Ándenle!* Get off my lawn! You're smashing it!"

Rudy and Alex sat up, startled. From the driveway, an old man waved a cane as he trotted toward them. The man was wearing a 49ers T-shirt and an L.A. Raiders cap.

"Let's split, homes!" Rudy yelled.

They rose quickly and picked up the door piled with their rattling cans. Rudy lost his balance and dropped to a knee. He scrambled to his feet.

"Come on, Rudy!" Alex shouted. "He's after us, dude!"

Rudy looked over his shoulder. The man was wild with anger at the apparent trespassers.

"You hoods!" the man shouted. "Whatta you got there? Is it stolen? Are those my cans?"

Rudy and Alex took off without answering, and the man ran after them, just a few steps behind Rudy. Rudy could feel the man's hot breath on his shoulders. He could even smell the man's stench of cigarette smoke, he was so close. And once he felt the cane sting his shoulder. The man yelled, "Thieves!"

"Sir, we're not thieves. My aunt gave them to us," Rudy tried to explain over his shoulder while running and trying to hold the door upright.

"You're lying," the old man snarled.

"Honest, sir."

"Rudy's telling the truth," Alex said in a voice that was out of breath.

"Hey, Alex, don't use our real names."

"Oh yeah, that's not cool. Sorry, Rudy."

"Alex! Don't use my name. *Estúpido*, now he knows!"

The boys clammed up. They strained to keep the door balanced. But when they took a corner, one of the trash bags toppled from the door. Rudy thought of stopping to get it, but the man was still right behind them. They left the bag with its guts of crushed soda cans spilling out.

The man gave up, slowing to a walk but shaking a fist at the boys. He yelled for them to stay out of his neighborhood.

They cashed in the aluminum soda cans, pocketing seventeen crisp new dollar bills. This put smiles back on their sweaty faces. They bought a soda on the way home after they sold the door for six dollars at the urban recycling center.

"We're cleaning up, homes," Rudy said. "Let's get something to eat."

"Yeah, let's get a pie."

They bought a lemon pie, which they gouged with their dirty fingers. They ate hungrily at a curb. Now and then Rudy glanced over his shoulder for the old man.

"Six for doing the doghouse and cleaning the garage. Seventeen for the cans. Six more for the door. Couple of bucks for cleaning up the *gatitos*," Rudy counted on his sticky fingers. "We're making out like bandits."

"*Híjole*, we're getting rich in America." Alex smiled. "My dad always said I'd get rich."

Rudy swallowed a clot of pie and licked his fingers. "Man, if someone broke something of mine, I'd understand. But not Slinky. I think he just likes to fight."

"Yeah, he's bad news."

That night, while Rudy was cooling his tired body in the three-ring inflatable pool in the yard, he got a call from his *nina*. He tiptoed inside the house, dripping. He picked up the telephone and heard his *nina* ask, "Rudy, do you know what happened to that door in the garage?"

"The door?" Rudy asked innocently. "What door?"

His *nina* described the door right down to the blistered paint and three drips of green paint on the doorknob. She mentioned that it was an antique door that she was going to have fitted in her house. Rudy, not knowing what to say, remarked, "Oh, that door, *nina*. Me and Alex borrowed it."

"I need it back, *mi'jo*," his *nina* said.

"Don't worry, *nina*. It's right here," he said. Rudy knocked on the door in the hallway. "Can you hear it?" Rudy held the phone to the door and knocked again. "I'll get it back to you tomorrow."

He hung up with his heart beating. "*Híjole*, I'm in trouble." For punishment, he knocked his forehead against the hallway door, kind of hard.

Chapter **3**

When they returned to the urban recycling center, Rudy and Alex discovered that the door they had sold for six dollars now cost twenty dollars. No matter how they begged and pleaded, no matter how they explained that the door belonged to Rudy's *nina* and that he was in big trouble, the clerk picked his teeth with a toothpick and muttered, "*Veinte dólares, pocho.*"

"But it belongs to my *nina*!"

"*Pues*, have your *nina* pick it up. I'll give her a good buy."

In the end, Rudy pushed his hands into his pockets, forked over the twenty, and grumbled all the way to his *nina*'s house. They propped the door in the garage, played with Curly for a while, and left. Dejected, they wandered over to a mall, where they bought a bag of popcorn and looked in shop windows.

"That was cold," Alex muttered, his cheek bulging with popcorn.

Rudy and Alex stood in front of a sporting goods store admiring the cleats and mitts. A cardboard cut-out of Barry Bonds smiled at them. He seemed to be making fun of them.

"Real cold," Rudy agreed.

"He shoulda just let you have the door back for nothin'. What was it to him?"

"I know. Now I only have a little more than ten bucks."

Rudy felt like crying and would have, except when he looked up, he spotted Slinky spitting a mouthful of sunflower seed shells. He would save his tears for later, for when Slinky thrashed him. Sneering, Slinky jumped on his lowered sixteen-inch bike, popped a wheelie, and rushed toward them. Rudy tugged on Alex's shirt and screamed, "It's Slinky. He saw us!"

Rudy and Alex dropped their popcorn, which scattered like snow, and ran out of the mall. They pumped their legs hard, as if they were running like Barry Bonds toward first base. They were almost overtaken when a hefty-looking security guard yanked Slinky off his bike. When the boys looked back, Slinky was waving a fist at them. They ran, walked, ran, and walked for nearly a mile, with spears of exhaustion jabbing their ribs. They walked in silence, their heads drooping like dead flowers. They jumped when they heard a harsh voice say, "Hey, you little creep!" For a split second, they thought it was Slinky. But it was another older kid calling another little creep.

They wandered down the alley, careful not to be seen, and threw themselves on a pile of stacked and yellowing newspapers. They sat in silence, each reflecting on his fleeting life.

"Do you think it's better to move to Mexico? I have relatives in Guadalajara," Rudy remarked after a moment of silence. He hadn't been this scared since he was four years old and had climbed onto the garage roof and couldn't get down. He had to stay there, crying up a lather of dirty tears, until his sister came home to help him down.

"Nah, we better just let Slinky beat you up," Alex responded coolly.

"Ah, man, you're cold."

"Just joking, Rudy." Alex smiled.

Rudy picked up one of the yellowed newspapers. He started reading a story about a man whose parachute didn't open, but lived to tell the tale because he landed on a mountain of snow. He read the article, his lips moving in disbelief. He rattled the newspaper at Alex and said, "If this dude can fall out of an airplane and live, then we get can get a job and save our lives."

"What are you talkin' about?" a sleepy Alex groaned with his eyes closed. The heat was making him drowsy. His eyes fluttered open. He looked around and rose slowly to his feet. "I got to go. Keep your eyes peeled for Slinky." He started up the alley and then turned and while walking backward yelled, "See you tomorrow. Stay strong, *carnal*!"

"Thanks, Alex."

Rudy sat on the pile of newspapers, reading the comics. Bored, he tossed the newspapers aside and rose to his feet with a tired grunt.

On his way home, he saw a flyer tacked on a telephone pole: LOST CAT. Tiptoeing, he read the description of an orange-colored cat with a mustache of white. The cat's name was Pudding, but it responded to Bud, Buddy, Pretty Face, and Principe.

"The cat's gotta lot of personalities," Rudy muttered to himself and ripped off the poster. He left, reading the description over and over, especially the part about the fifty-dollar reward.

"What luck," he said under his breath. He tried to remember where he last saw a cat that fit the description. Most of the cats he knew were gray or shades of gray. He plucked two apricots from a limb hanging over the fence, rubbed them on his shirt, and broke them in half to eat. He stopped his chewing when he heard a meow. A striped cat was batting a half-dead mouse.

"You mean cat!" Rudy scolded. "Leave that *ratoncito* alone." Rudy threw a rock at the cat, who leaped and ran away. The mouse wiggled away to freedom.

Rudy spent the rest of the morning and afternoon looking for the lost cat. He beat the bushes around his street and called out "Pudding, Bud, Buddy, Pretty Face, Principe" until his throat was hoarse. He found a whole neighborhood of cats. He found a black cat with a white mustache. He found a brown cat, a black cat, one cat without a tail, one cat with a nibbled ear, one mother cat with a litter of six kittens. But he couldn't find the orange cat with a white mustache.

Rudy gave up and returned home. He grubbed on a peanut butter tortilla warmed on a burner and drank Kool-Aid that left purple stains around his mouth. He turned on the television, but turned it off when he saw there was nothing on except *telenovelas*. He pulled out the lost cat flyer crumpled in his pocket and telephoned the number at the bottom. On the third ring, a woman answered, "Hellooooo."

"Hello, I'm calling about Pudding," Rudy said.

"Pudding? Did you find him?" the woman asked in a rushed voice.

"No, but I'm looking. Does the cat really go by all those names?"

"Yes, and sometimes we call him Tuna."

The woman told Rudy the reward was now sixty-five dollars. His eyes widened when he heard this figure. He told the woman that he would find her for sure, even though it might take a day or two. Next he dialed Mrs. Estrada, the woman with thirteen cats. When she answered the telephone, he could hear, even over the babbling of the television, the army of cats tumbling and fighting in the background.

"Mrs. Estrada, it's me—Rudy!" Rudy screamed into the mouthpiece.

"*¿Quién?*" Mrs. Estrada screamed back. "*Espérate.* Wait a minute." She muffled the telephone, clapped her hands, and yelled to a cat, "Spanky, get off the television. Quit changing the channel." The cat was pressing her paws on the remote control. She then came back on the telephone and repeated, "*¿Quién es?*"

"It's me, Rudy. I helped you comb your cats," Rudy explained.

"Ah, *sí*," Mrs. Estrada said brightly. "You and your friend did a good job. The cats stopped scratching."

"That's cool," Rudy said. "I was wondering if you could help me."

"What for?"

"Can you tell me how to catch a lost cat?"

"Es posible. ¿Qué pasó?"

Rudy explained the flyer that was posted near his house, and he described the cat.

"You know, *mi'jo,* that cat sounds like I seen him before. You mean kind of orange with a little *bigote*?"

"Yeah, that's him. That's the dude!"

"Pues, I think he was in the backyard with Tomas and Louie."

"Your sons?"

"No, they're my cats."

"That's great. Thanks." Rudy hung up, grinning ear to ear so that the tops of his gums showed. He rubbed his palms together like a fly and buzzed, "I'm saved!"

Rudy hurried over to Mrs. Estrada's house. He found her on the front porch, trying to nudge a cat from the window screen with a broom.

"¡Ándale! Get down," she hollered. She stomped her foot and yelled, *"¡Gatito maldito!"*

The cat hissed on the screen and climbed higher.

"Mrs. Estrada, it's me," Rudy said.

Mrs. Estrada turned around, squinted one eye at Rudy, and recognizing him, smiled her toothless smile. She put down the broom and said, "*¡Ven acá!* Come inside!" To the kitten clinging to the screen, she snapped, "You gonna fall if you keep goofin' around."

As Rudy stepped into the living room, he saw a big cat pounce on a little one and others running around the house. A kitten was on the dining table, licking an empty cereal bowl. Mrs. Estrada clapped her hands, and the cats scattered.

"Now"—she sighed—"what about this lost cat?"

Rudy again described the cat while Mrs. Estrada sprinkled fish food in her aquarium. She nodded her head as she listened. Then she stopped listening.

"Buster is probably hungry too," she said under her breath.

"Who's Buster?"

"I never showed you Buster? Come with me," she said, scooting back the chair as she rose to her feet. She prodded a hesitant Rudy to her back bedroom. He made out a bubbling sound and then a purplish glow that cast shadows on the wall. On a table sat an aquarium, where a huge bass floated slowly, its wisps of nearly transparent fins rowing to keep afloat.

"¡Chihuahua! It's huge. It can hardly move," Rudy said as he dropped to his knees. He rapped the glass with his knuckle, clicked his tongue, and sang, "Hey, Buster, ¿qué pasa?"

As Buster swam in profile, the bass's nose touched the front of the glass, and his tail swished the back. His eyes looked droopy, and his fat lip pouted.

"You must have had him a long time," Rudy said.

"Six years. He was this big when I got him." Mrs. Estrada spread a space between her thumb and index finger. "He needs to go in the other direction." She dipped her hands into the water, brought out the dripping fish, and turned him the other way. She explained that once a week she changed his direction. She imagined that he must get bored going one way. She tossed a handful of fish food on the water and threw a kiss at Buster.

Right then, as he got to his feet, Rudy decided that he had better not ask Mrs. Estrada for advice. She's weird, Rudy thought, una loca. He backed away from the aquarium and out of the bedroom. He told Mrs. Estrada that he had to go home and mow his lawn. When he descended the front steps, the kitten was still clinging to the window screen. He hissed at Rudy, and then hissed at Mrs. Estrada, who came out with a squirt gun. She waved good-bye and proceeded to blast the kitten from the screen.

Rudy hurried away. He decided to find some honest work under the blazing Fresno sun.

Chapter **4**

Rudy stood at the end of a line of heavy-set mariachis, gripping a pair of reddish maracas in one hand. He was sweaty from standing under the glare of lights. He put his lips around the straw in his soda, his cheeks collapsing on a hard suck. He looked over at his Tío Jaime, who was tapping the mouthpiece of his trumpet against his palm.

"*Pues*, Little Rudy, you play good," his *tío* said. He smiled, revealing gold-trimmed front teeth. His eyes were watery and looked, to

Rudy, like they might begin to cry at any moment.

When Rudy had taken a bubble bath, combed his hair, and splashed himself with cologne, his parents became suspicious.

"What's this about you wanting to work?" his father asked.

"There's money to be made, Dad," Rudy had answered after a moment of hesitation. He wanted to tell him about Slinky, but bit his tongue in two places to keep from talking. He figured he would scream for his parents' help only when Slinky had him in a headlock.

Hired to play in a wedding, his uncle had added Rudy to his group, Los Mariachis del Sol. His uncle had hired him out of kindness—he didn't really need a boy to shake out the wrong beat. Rudy knew this but didn't care. His uncle was paying him ten dollars. And he was going to let Rudy take up a paper plate and help himself to *pollo con mole*, the traditional wedding meal that splotched shirts and dresses.

"Am I really playing good?" Rudy asked.

The musicians smiled, and the guitarist remarked in Spanish, "You have a future, young man. I suggest the *guitarrón*."

Rudy turned his attention to his *tío*, who was muttering to his players, *"Tu recuerdo y yo,"* a *ranchera*. The musicians raised their instruments. The song began with a flush of notes, and the crowd took to the dance floor. Rudy pumped his maracas and added his voice, sounding more like a baby bird fallen from a tree than a true mariachi.

Rudy noticed an older couple, their bodies pressed together, turning like tops. They danced cheek-to-cheek while the other dancers made room for them. As Rudy looked over the crowd of dancers, his gaze fell upon a clot of kids his age, all leaning against the wall. They were sipping sodas and eating seeds. He slowed his maracas to a chug, throwing off the *guitarrón* player, who narrowed his eyes at Rudy. He slowed to a stop and let his mouth hang open.

"It's Slinky," Rudy mumbled to himself. He thought, What is he doing here?

Rudy glanced toward the exit. For a second, he thought of jumping off the stage but decided to take his chances right where he was, next to his uncle.

Slinky crushed a paper cup in his fist and swaggered toward the bandstand. He stood,

hands curled, in front of Rudy. After a long, hard gaze that could have cut diamonds, Slinky with a ratlike smirk said, "*Sapo*, I'm going to get you!"

"What are you doing here?" Rudy asked.

"It's my sister's wedding."

"I thought she was married."

"Shut up, *sapo*. I hate your face." He spat out some sunflower seed shells. Slinky punched his fist into his palm and threatened, "Your head is going to rattle like those maracas." He returned to lean against the wall with his friends. They pointed at Rudy and laughed.

All night Rudy played the maracas and looked out for Slinky. On one song he strummed the guitar chords he knew—G, C, and E. Now he could see why his *tío*'s eyes were sad. The songs were sad, even the lively ones.

"Rudy," his *tío* called at the end of "Tequila." He tossed him his car keys. "I want you to go the car and look in the glove compartment. Get me the Vaseline." His *tío* touched his puckered lips, which were swollen.

"Okay, *tío*," Rudy said as he examined the

car keys, which hung on a toy trumpet. He worked the taps up and down. He blew on the trumpet and out squeaked a noise.

Rudy jumped off the stage. When he looked over to the wall where Slinky had stood, he saw only three balloons taped to the wall. Slinky and his group were gone.

Rudy walked among the crowd. The bride and groom were cutting the cake, their hands linked together over the knife. The bride fed her groom a piece, and then shoved it in hard so that his mustache bristled with the frosting. The crowd laughed, and Rudy's mouth began to water. The cake looked good.

Rudy recognized Sara Cano, a girl from school. She was dancing by herself. When she looked up and saw Rudy watching her, she ran away, nearly knocking over the bride and groom. Rudy shrugged his shoulders and mused, "I guess she doesn't like me."

In the parking lot, Rudy found the car. He unlocked the door, climbed in, and began to search for the jar of Vaseline among the clutches of bills, fuses, wrenches, screwdrivers, chewed pencils, parking tickets, and expired dog tags. He found the jar and was leaving when he heard footsteps over gravel.

He looked in the rearview mirror and eye-balled Slinky walking toward the car.

"Ah, man," Rudy whispered to himself. He locked the door just as Slinky's hand wrapped around the handle.

"Get outta the car!" Slinky shouted. He pressed his face against the glass so that his nostrils flared and he left a blotch of hot breathing.

"No!"

"I said get out!"

"I said no."

"I won't hurt you. I promise!" Slinky smiled through his packed teeth, changing his tune.

"*¡Chale!* You're lying."

Slinky's smile dropped into an angry scowl. He pounded the window, shouting for Rudy to get out and take his beating like a good fourth grader.

Without much thought, Rudy fit the car keys into the ignition and turned over the engine. A bone of fear lodged in his throat. He pressed the accelerator with the ball of his shoe, the engine roaring and drowning out Slinky's threats. He put it into gear. Rudy slowly pulled away, and Slinky began to run after the car, showering it with handfuls of gravel.

"What am I doing?" Rudy asked himself. He maneuvered the car halfway up the street when he remembered to turn on the headlights. He pulled a switch, and the wipers began to clack across the windshield. He pulled a knob, and a vent began to blow air into his face. He pulled another knob, and this time the headlights came on, a pale light fanning against the black asphalt. The headlights caught the eyes of an orange cat crossing the street. The cat stopped momentarily in the road, then scurried into a junglelike yard.

"It's the lost cat!" Rudy shouted to himself. For a second, Rudy pictured a woman counting out his reward money in ten-dollar bills and piling them in his hands. He then pictured himself piling them into Slinky's outstretched palm.

Rudy looked momentarily into the rearview mirror but kept his attention on the road. Once his mother had let him steer the car while she was driving, and another time he had driven his cousin Lalo's go-cart. But his uncle's car was different. His feud with Slinky was taking a serious turn.

"*Híjole*, I'm in big trouble," Rudy moaned to himself. He reached for the blinkers to make a turn, but instead he sprayed the windshield with water and the wipers moved faster. The bugs on the windshield began to smear.

Rudy drove around the block and guided his uncle's car back to the parking lot. He decided that it would be better if Slinky just beat him up than to get caught by the police or, worse, his *tío* Jaime. How could he ever explain why he had taken the car, he a ten-year-old with good grades and nice parents?

"It was a short life, and a pretty good one," Rudy said as the car climbed up the driveway into the parking lot. He had swallowed that bone of fear and felt that it—his ten years on this planet—was over. But when he parked the car and got out to face his whipping, Slinky was no longer in sight. Except for the cars and two men sitting on the steps of the hall, the parking lot was empty.

"Where did he go?" Rudy asked, his heart beating under his white shirt. He gripped the jar of Vaseline and opened it. He smeared his own lips, which were raw from his nervous biting. He capped the jar and returned to the hall. His *tío*, huge as a bear, was hovering over a plate of *pollo con mole*.

"Where you been?" Tío asked after he cleared his throat. "*¿Qué pasó?* You find that girl?"

"What girl?"

"Hey, *hombre*, that little girl who's been making eyes at you all night."

Rudy looked around the dance floor. His uncle must have meant Sara Cano.

"*¿Tienes hambre?* You hungry?" Uncle asked.

Rudy shook his head and handed his uncle the jar of Vaseline. "Just thirsty."

His *tío* pointed with his fork in the direction of the punch bowl. Rudy drank like a camel, long and hard, before he climbed back onto the stage. He nervously scanned the crowd, but Slinky was nowhere in sight.

After their gig, the mariachis packed their instruments into their van. It was near midnight. The traffic light, Rudy could see, was already blinking red red red red.

"That's funny. I thought I parked over there," Tío said as he walked over the gravel to his car. He was confused. He was certain that he had parked by the Dumpster, but now his car was sitting next to a dusty green Ford. He shrugged his shoulders and got into the car. When he turned over the engine, the blinkers, the windshield wipers, the radio, and the vent all went on at once.

"¡Ay, Dios!" his uncle screamed, springing from the car.

"Is something wrong?" Rudy asked, eyes wide with feigned innocence.

His suspicious *tío* shook his head at Rudy, who smiled a disarming smile and said, "Tío Jaime, you play really good!"

Chapter **5**

Rudy leaned against the sink and let the soapsuds crawl up his arm. He was scrubbing baby bottles with a bristle brush. He poked the brush into the bottle, and when he plunged it up and down, rainbowlike bubbles floated lazily up and over the dish rack. He looked out the kitchen window. On the sill, an avocado pit lanced with toothpicks sat in a jar of water. Rudy began to examine his ten-year-old life. He had worked some fairly odd jobs: combed cats, repaired a doghouse, hauled aluminum cans, and shaken out sweet rhythms in a mariachi group. He wondered how his father, a construction worker, could wake every day and face the blistering sun. His mother took phone orders at a meat factory all day. Work was hard and getting harder for his family. Now he was baby-sitting his *tía*'s year-old twins while Tía went to a day game of bingo.

"Man, I better make some money pretty soon," he said to himself. He played inside his head the image of Slinky's hate-filled face caught in the rearview mirror. Rudy shivered and looked around for the soap bubbles. They were gone, all popped against the hard edges of spoons and forks.

The twin babies came tottering into the kitchen. Their tiny fists were curled around crayons. Rudy noticed that one of them, Lalo he thought, was chewing on a crayon.

"Let me have it," Rudy begged, dropping to his knee. The last thing he wanted to do was get in trouble with his *tía*.

The baby smiled a toothless smile. Rudy could see a slug of chewed crayon in the back of his mouth—aquamarine blue. With clean hands, Rudy prodded the crayon from the baby's mouth. Immediately, baby Lalo began to cry, two fat tears rolling from his eyes and splashing Rudy's knuckles. Rudy was amazed at how hot they were.

"You're not supposed to eat crayons," Rudy told the baby. *"¡Es cochino!"*

Rudy picked Lalo up and rocked him in his arms. The baby quieted for a second and then began crying more hot tears when he saw his bottles in the dish rack.

"You hungry?" Rudy asked, patting the baby's arm. He let the baby slide from his arms and filled the bottle with grape Kool-Aid. He filled a second bottle for the other baby, Nati, who was peeling the paper from his crayon. He led them by their tiny hands to the living room, each of them sucking on their bottles.

"You little diaper dudes!" Rudy screamed.

He stood facing a wall scribbled with loops of the aquamarine blue crayon and fiery tangles of mandarin orange. The babies gazed up at Rudy, their pinkish cheeks swiftly pumping the cool purple Kool-Aid.

"Pretty," one of the twins said brightly.

"Pretty ugly," Rudy countered.

With a dab of Dutch cleanser and a washcloth, Rudy scrubbed the wall as best he could. He worked the towel over the scribbles, holding back from scolding the twins. Just as he was finishing, he heard his name— "Rudy."

Rudy winced at the twins, who turned their large heads toward the front window. For a moment, Rudy thought one of them was talking, and he began to wonder how a baby could sound like an older kid so suddenly.

"Rudy! *¡Menso!*" he heard again. He craned his neck toward the front window. He thought it was his father, but it was Alex, peering in with his hands around his face. He tapped on the glass, and Rudy rose from his knees.

"How did you know I was here?" Rudy asked when he answered the door.

"Your mom told me."

"She's at work."

"Nah, she came home for something." Alex studied the crayon-tortured wall and remarked, "Real Picassos."

"All I do is clean up after them," Rudy lamented. "Especially Lalo."

"Which one is Lalo? They look the same to me."

"The one with crayon in his mouth!"

Again Rudy had to fall on his knee and probe the crayon from Lalo's mouth.

While Rudy worked on Lalo, Nati crawled off the couch and offered Alex his bottle. "Bop-bop," the baby squealed as he shook his bottle. "Bop-bop."

"Thanks, dude," Alex said, ruffling Nati's hair, "but I had mine with Cheerios." To Rudy he said excitedly, "Listen, I got another idea how you can make some money."

"I got one too. *Mi tía* said I can sell the apricots from her tree." He pointed vaguely to the backyard. "What's your idea?"

"Well, it's kind of strange."

"What is it?"

"Well," Alex said, hesitating. "I thought maybe we could dress up like Aztec dancers and stand on a corner."

"You're kidding."

"*En serio*, man," Alex answered. "My brother does that in college when he needs some *feria*."

"Does he make money?"

"All the time. He just sticks feathers on his *cola* and hops around like a bird with one leg."

"I think we better sell the apricots," Rudy

said after a moment of thought. He didn't like the idea of standing half-naked in his *chones* on a street corner. Who knows who would see him?

While the twins sat on the lawn pulling up fistfuls of grass, Rudy and Alex poked their faces in the lower branches of the apricot tree. They pulled at the fruit, soft and tender to the point of gushing juice, and threw them into a bag. They filled bag after bag and helped themselves to the juicy ones.

"They're pretty good," Alex said.

"I like them more hard, not so soft," Rudy said. He spat a pit at Alex, and Alex spat one back at Rudy. The pit landed inside Rudy's shirt. He screamed, "Two points, homes," and wiggled his T-shirt until the pit rolled down his chest to his belly and onto the ground.

Rudy rolled a few in the direction of the baby twins, who rose and tottered curiously toward the fruit. They bit into them and spat the pits onto the lawn.

While Alex carried the babies in his arms, Rudy carried the five bags of apricots to the front yard. They set up a fruit stand on the lawn and sat in the shade eating apricots. Before long, an older woman came by pushing a grocery cart. She stopped, looked at the boys, and then asked as she took in the bags of fruit, "What are you asking for them?"

"Five apricots for ten cents," the boys answered. "That's two cents an apricot."

The woman thought about it for a while before she said, "You're good at math. How 'bout we make a trade?"

"What do you want to trade?" Alex asked, suddenly interested. "You got any soda in the cart?"

"I'll trade you a load of homegrown squash."

"Squash? You mean . . . vegetables?" Rudy asked, his face twisted in horror. The only vegetable he liked was cucumbers, and then only in a salad.

"Yeah," the woman said, peeking into the paper bags. "I grow them myself. Everyone loves my squash."

"*Señora*, I'm sorry, but I don't like squash," Rudy confessed politely.

The woman pleaded, the three moles on her chin wiggling from her excitement. She explained the vitamin content of one average-length squash. She smacked her lips and assured the boys that her squash was sweet-tasting. In the end, the boys shrugged their shoulders and relented.

The woman helped herself to handfuls of apricots, and the boys, in turn, gathered an armful of thorny squash from her cart.

"They're good, huh?" Rudy said as he watched the woman nibble one, her mouth moving as rapidly as a squirrel's.

"A bit ripe. Not good for canning. But I'm going to use them in cookies." She ate the meat of the fruit and spat the seed out—far.

"You make cookies?" Rudy asked.

"Not only are you good at math, you're a comedian," the woman chuckled. "Of course I make cookies. I'm a grandma. In fact, I sell them out of my house. Here." The woman rifled through one of her bags and brought out a single oatmeal cookie. She snapped it in half and gave pieces to Rudy and Alex. She licked her fingertips and pushed her hand back into the bag. She brought out two more for Lalo and Nati, who took them and turned them over like coins. They began to munch away.

"Listen," she proposed to the boys, "how about if I trade you my cookies for your apricots?"

Rudy felt uneasy about this. He remembered his mother's warnings that you shouldn't take candy from strangers, and perhaps, he thought, this warning included cookies. Still, he couldn't help himself. The trade seemed fair, and the woman seemed nice enough.

"How many cookies you got?" Rudy asked.

"One bag."

"Only one bag?" Alex asked. "Doesn't seem fair."

"Doesn't seem fair!" she scolded, eyes flashing with flames of anger. "You know how much electricty and gas cost? And butter, and my time?"

"How much?" Rudy asked lamely.

"Lots. *¡Mucho dinero!*" the woman shouted.

Rudy and Alex jumped at the scolding and said, "All right, all right! Just give us a minute."

Rudy and Alex huddled together.

"No one is going to buy these apricots. They're too soft," Alex whispered. "It's too hot out here."

"Yeah, you're probably right," Rudy concurred. "It's better than nothing."

They made the exchange. They placed the

bags of apricots in her cart while she dangled the bag of cookies between her thumb and index finger. "I hope you enjoy them," she sang.

"We will," Rudy smiled.

"Try the squash in tomato sauce," the woman advised as she started to leave, the wheels of her cart squeaking.

The boys sat on the lawn. They ate three cookies each and gave two to the twins, who instead of sitting in the shade were now in the sun. They looked hot. They moved the babies into the shade, where they sprayed them with the garden hose. They quickly cooled off.

"Hey, look, Rudy," Alex said. Alex was pointing at the squash, which had little chunks missing. "I think they've been eating the squash."

Rudy examined the teeth marks. He looked at them for the longest time and, tossing the squash aside, concluded, "I think these teeth *marcas* belong to Lalo."

They lounged on the lawn, finished the remaining cookies, and thought about their trade.

"Man, I think we got taken," Rudy said. "She got the better deal."

"Yeah," Alex agreed. "The cookies weren't

even any good. They tasted like they didn't have any sugar in them. They sort of tasted like squash."

The babies began to cry big tears. The boys hustled them inside for a nap and set themselves in front of the television to watch a rerun of *The Simpsons*. They needed to forget their troubles and laugh for a while.

eed any good? They used it that way once, to keep the intruders away. They put up fences to unmark...

The bobcat, when he was big, came out of the cage, but made him run for a bar, and set them free. In front of all the crowd, came to watch him run as the two strangers made a rush to free their wild life up for a while.

Chapter **6**

Once a month, Rudy's grandpa, El Shorty, arrived in his rattling Chevy truck. He drove from Pismo Beach, where he had settled after retiring, spending his days fishing or bartering at the local swap meet. He came for dinner and to sharpen any cutting implements at Rudy's household. He would bring out his whetstone and sharpen the sewing scissors, kitchen knives, and even the chrome-plated toenail clippers. He would whistle while he worked, his hat tilted back on his head, his face glistening. He sharpened the garden hoe and the pruning shears. He sharpened the hatchet and the alligator-toothed saw. He set the lawn mower on a bench and sharpened the blades until they cut paper as efficiently as scissors.

Today El Shorty came over just when Rudy felt a great dread weight on his bony shoulders. Though he desperately needed a job, he couldn't find one. He had looked and looked, even following the leads in the classified ads. He had read one ad about working on a freighter. Rudy had liked that idea; he might board a freighter to the South Pacific and return when he was older, a tattoo on each arm and one on his muscled chest. Then he could take care of Slinky without the help of any older cousins. But he knew this was only a kid's desperate dream. He wasn't going to the South Pacific. He wasn't going anywhere, except maybe into the ground if Slinky caught him.

To make matters worse, Alex was grounded for setting off a firecracker while his mother and a *tía* were in the kitchen talking up *chisme*. His mother was dunking a doughnut into her coffee when the firecracker exploded. Alex wouldn't be around for two days—a long time to be without the help of a friend, Rudy concluded.

El Shorty's work was finished. He sat in the shade of the grape arbor sharpening a pearl-handled pocketknife. He was whistling the theme song to *Bonanza*, a really old television show.

"Grandpa," Rudy whispered as he stood at his side.

"*¿Qué quieres, mi'jo?*" El Shorty said without looking up.

"I need your advice. I'm in trouble."

El Shorty's watery eyes rose and stared at his grandson. He put his whetstone down and folded the pocketknife, which he slipped into his shirt pocket. His work-hardened hands lay in his lap.

"I broke this guy's Discman," Rudy confessed. When his grandfather's brow knitted in confusion, Rudy made a square shape with his hands and explained, "A Discman is like a radio. Like a Walkman, Grandpa."

Rudy explained to his grandfather how he had broken it, right down to the feeling when his knee busted the plastic. He told him about Slinky, a *vato loco*, and how he and Alex, his number one *carnal*, had gotten a number of "odd" jobs, from baby-sitting to playing in a mariachi band.

His grandfather thought for a moment. He scratched his neck and confessed, "You know, Little Rudy, I had the same problem *en México. Pero* it was about a top, *un trompo.*"

El Shorty told Rudy a story about how as a boy, he had borrowed his friend's wooden top for a local tournament. It was a special top, one that could spin a really long time, longer than any other top in their *pueblo.* But during the tournament he saw a boy with a top that danced and bumped better than any he had ever seen. The boy was rich. He was snotty and full of confidence. El Shorty explained to Rudy his envy, his desperation to win.

"I felt the pressure from the people watching, the people from my town," El Shorty said. "When my last turn came, I flicked the top so hard that it cracked into two, like lightning had struck it."

"Mala suerte," Rudy sighed.

"¡Es verdad! I had broken my friend's top, which was so beautiful. *Como una fruta,* round and perfect."

"What did you do, Grandpa?"

"Pues, I made him a new one."

El Shorty then explained that that was how he had learned to whittle, and because of that to sharpen knives. He located the heart of a felled ash tree and, with the help of his own grandfather, Don Luis Hernandez, whittled it into a top. He sanded the top until it was perfectly balanced and then painted it the colors of the Mexican flag—green, white, and red, with an eagle clutching a snake.

"You made a top from nothing?" Rudy asked, amazed. Once he had tried to sharpen a stick with a knife but only ended up shaving his finger like a carrot.

"It was not from nothing. It was from a tree," El Shorty said, his hands flying up.

"But I can't make a Discman, Grandpa."

"No, you can't. But you must give back something in return." El Shorty drank from his water glass and smacked his lips. "So this boy is after you?"

"Yeah. He told me to get out of town or else."

"*Cuidado.* I don't think you should provoke this *chamaco.* Let him alone."

"I wish he would leave me alone," Rudy said. After a moment he said, "You got in fights when you were a boy, didn't you, Grandpa. I heard some of your stories."

"*¡Claro que sí!* I had my share of fights when I was a boy," Grandpa responded with a smile. He touched his forehead, which was pleated with wrinkles, and said proudly, "I have a few lumps to prove it. But it's not the right thing to do."

"You fought a lot?"

"No, not many times. But I remember one fight with Javier Gonzalez. He was a very good soccer player and a good talker with the girls. We got in an argument not over soccer or girls but about shining shoes."

"Shining shoes!"

"Yes, when I was a boy, I shined shoes. I was very good, I must say. You might want to try that."

"What happened?"

"Javier tried to take over my corner."

El Shorty explained that in Mexico the boys would claim a street corner. That corner was yours until you gave up shining shoes and moved on to another job.

"It was a very good corner," El Shorty said. "It was in front of a clothing store. It had an awning that provided shade. *Pues,* then Javier showed up and told me to go away."

El Shorty then raised his fists in a boxing stance and growled, "I told him, 'Javier, you better leave or else.'"

He chuckled as he lowered his fists. He said that he must have been a funny sight because Javier was older and big as a *burro* and just as dumb.

"So you fought him?" Rudy asked.

"Fought him! We boxed from a little before noon all the way to dark, that's how much I was upset!" Eyes narrowed in anger, El Shorty jabbed and pawed the air. "I hit him with a left, then a right, and circled him *como un gallo,* like a rooster."

Rudy gave his grandfather a questioning look. He could see in El Shorty's eyes that there was a little exaggeration.

"*Pues,* the truth is, we pushed each other a couple of times, and then he left with his shoe-shine box under his arm. He wasn't really a bad rascal." El Shorty took another drink from his water glass and then, patting Rudy's shoulder, said, "I think it's best if you stay away from this boy. He's only trouble."

"But we—Alex and me—can't find any real jobs."

"You don't need a job, *mi'jo*."

"How am I going to get some money to buy the Discman?"

El Shorty took another drink from his water glass and reflected darkly on this question. His eyes brightened as he clapped his hands.

"*Mira*, in Pismo Beach, I fish for a little extra money. I have an extra pole in my truck." He rose stiffly from his chair, and together they went to the front yard, where Rudy's grandfather unlocked a box and brought out a fishing pole. He connected it and attached a weight to the line. He began instructing Rudy on how to cast his line.

"Just a little zip from your wrist. *Nada más*," El Shorty said with his hand over Rudy's. "Look at the spot where you want your sinker to land."

Rudy looked at the front lawn, still wet from a morning watering. He dreamed up a river with loads of twelve-inch trout. He cast his fishing pole, the line snapping out in a tangle. He cast a second time, then a third. He got better and better, a whistle on his lips.

"That's very nice," his grandfather sang.

"Now just think of the pole as a part of your arm."

Rudy practiced until the flight of his line and sinker were effortless and, for a boy of ten, a thing of beauty. Only one time did he cast his sinker into the tree. Only one time did his line get tangled in the hedge.

"*Perfecto*," his grandfather chimed.

When his mother called them in to dinner, Rudy put his fishing pole away in the garage.

That night they had fishsticks—six for the grown-ups and five each for Rudy and his sister Estela. Right there, ideas began to swim like fish inside his head. Everyone likes fish, Rudy thought to himself. He figured he could catch some and sell them. He cut a fishstick and let the steam curl around his fork. He blew on it and devoured it in three hungry bites from his gleaming fork.

Chapter 7

In the early morning, Rudy and Alex bicycled out of town with their fishing poles and a bucket with three earthworms. Rudy was going to follow his grandfather's advice: to keep away from Slinky and reel in loads of fish. A radio swung on Rudy's handlebars. A lunch of tuna sandwiches, wrapped in a plastic bread bag, swung on Alex's handlebars. The boys headed at breakneck speed toward Minkler. They were determined to wrestle the river of trout, bluegill, and possibly some nasty-looking mustached catfish.

They arrived in Minkler just before noon, hot and sticky, their legs ragged from the long ride. When they sat down in the shade of a mulberry, sweat flooded every fold and crevice on their bodies.

"This heat is ugly," Rudy growled as he took off his T-shirt and fanned his brown belly.

"I didn't know I had this much water in me," Alex agreed. He lay down and let the sweat pool in his belly button. After a while he rose up with a push of his hands. "Rudy, you ever notice that when you drink milk, you sweat water?"

"Yeah, it's weird," Rudy agreed. "I remember when I drank orange Kool-Aid all day, and it came out just clear." He smashed an ant climbing up his arm. "Biology is weird."

After a short rest, Rudy and Alex locked their bikes to a tree and walked toward the river. They stepped through a booby trap of what they imagined to be poison ivy. They tripped and fell and laughed at themselves because they knew they were *barrio* kids, with *chicharrones*, not Huck Finn and Tom Sawyer.

The river ran swift and cool, and this made

them happy. A breeze blew across the rippling dark water. Some sparrows yakked in the cottonwood trees that shadowed the river. Far away, a dog barked and whined.

"We're going to make a bundle," Rudy told Alex.

"You sure we can sell what we catch?"

"Yeah."

Alex picked up one of the worms, examined the three-inch-long creature, and wincing from the painful act, impaled it on the hook. The worm wiggled and squirmed at first, but then hung like a shoestring from the hook. "We can sell the fish to my uncle. He likes fish."

"What kind of fish is in here?" Rudy asked as he scanned the water's edge. He peered down at a rusty beer can and a soggy potato chip bag.

"Trout."

"You sure?"

"Trout, and maybe the kind they make fishsticks with."

"No kidding? I had fishsticks last night." He weighed his grandfather's fishing pole in his hands. It felt just right, like an extension of his arm. El Shorty would be proud, he thought, and reached for a wriggling worm.

Alex stepped toward the river and warned, "Here goes, homes!" With all his might, Alex cast his line out on the water. The hook and sinker dropped two feet in front of him. He tried a second time, and a third. With each cast, the hook and sinker landed a bit farther out, where the water rippled white against the rocks.

"I practiced with *mi abuelo*. Here goes mine," Rudy bragged as he looked over his shoulder at the end of his pole. He pulled out a yard of fishing line from the reel. He let his fishing pole swing over his head. But instead of a beautiful cast, his hook and sinker fell at his feet. He tried again, and this time it flew out far enough to scare up the fishes' interest.

The boys sat on the bank, their legs pulled to their chests. They drank water from their plastic bottle. They ate their tuna sandwiches and some apricots and chatted loudly. They talked about the most embarrassing moments in their lives. For Rudy, it was when he sneezed *mocos* after Frostie Gonzalez tackled him during recess. For Alex, it was when he flicked a spitball from the car while his father was driving down the freeway. The spitball landed on the cheek of the driver in the next lane. His father pulled the car over and made him apologize.

They talked and talked as their lines lay on the water without one tug. After a while, they reeled in their lines and saw that the hooks were clean.

"Man, the worms got away, homes," Rudy complained. A single drop of water clung to the needle of the fishhook.

They rebaited the hooks with *chicharrones* and recast their lines almost perfectly. They stared transfixed at the swift push of the current. As the afternoon got hotter, they batted away gnats and horseflies.

"These flies got teeth," Rudy complained as he bloodied a bug against his neck.

"De veras," Alex agreed. He slapped his cheek. When he pulled his hand away, a bloody mosquito lay pressed against his palm.

"Maybe we should get in the water. I think they're after our sweat."

"They can have it."

Giggling, the boys undressed down to their *chones* and slowly crawled into the icy river. Immediately, their bodies splotched with goosebumps. They shivered and hugged themselves. They yelled from the coldness, splashing at each other. But they stopped their play when they saw Rudy's fishing pole being yanked. A fish was on the end of his line. They scampered toward shore, their sagging underwear nearly falling off from the weight of water and silt.

"*¡Chihuahua!*" Rudy screamed as he picked up the pole and felt the weight of the struggling fish. "It's Moby Dick's great-great grandson. The dude's huge."

"It's Jaws's *abuelito*," Alex joked.

Rudy reeled and yanked and panted and yelled. The fish leaped from the water, tail thrashing, not ready to give up. Finally, the fish was landed, flopping on the bank's edge.

"He's big, *¿que no?*" Rudy asked.

"Real big. The guy musta been lifting weights or something."

The fish flopped until it was exhausted and completely covered with dirt. Then it stared pointlessly at the sky. Its mouth opened and closed like a fist, and its gills worked for air.

"You gonna take the hook out?" Rudy asked.

"*Chale.* I can't do it, homes."

"Come on, Alex."

"Nah, I'll faint. Besides, you caught the dude."

Sucking in good air to keep from fainting, Rudy bent down and, on one knee, swiftly pulled the hook from the fish's mouth. Both boys screamed from the apparent pain, and the fish began to wiggle on the ground.

"I got an idea," Rudy said as he gently picked up the fish. "¡Ándale! Let's get him back to town—alive."

"Why?" Alex asked, confused.

"I'll tell you on the way home."

Rudy placed him in the bucket with some river water. They got dressed and hurried from the river, nearly tripping in the sandy earth and spilling their catch. They unlocked their bikes and pushed them toward the main road. They flagged a truck down and asked for a ride back to town. The driver hooked a thumb and told them to get in the back.

"So what's your idea?" Alex asked.

In the back of the pickup, the wind ruffled their hair and caught their words and flung them far. They rocked over the slightest potholes. The pail between Rudy's legs sloshed water. "What?" he shouted. "I can't hear you!"

"I said, What's your idea?"

Rudy nodded his head. He explained that he was going to sell the fish, which he had named Fishstick, to Mrs. Estrada. She had a fish that was just as huge, and perhaps it needed a friend to hang out with.

"Good idea," Alex smiled. They slapped palms and thanked the saint of brown boys in trouble. Surely Mrs. Estrada would pay good bucks for a fish this size. Soon Slinky would be off their backs.

The boys were dropped off two blocks from Rudy's house. While Rudy returned the fishing poles to the garage, Alex refilled the bucket of water and tossed in a slice of bread for the fish to eat. Rudy's mother called from the kitchen window. Rudy pressed a finger to his pursed lips. The boys tiptoed around the back and over the fence when they heard his mother shout, "Rudy, I want you to pull the weeds in the flower bed. Rudy! *Ven acá.*"

They hurried over to Mrs. Estrada's house. She sat on the front steps cracking walnuts with the wrong side of a hatchet. A coffee can stood at her side.

"Mrs. Estrada!" Rudy called as he climbed halfway up her porch. He was a little nervous watching her work with a hatchet.

She looked up and tossed the meat of the walnut into her mouth. "Who is it?" she mumbled. "My grandsons?"

"No, it's us, your workers."

She rose with a grunt, slapping shells from her lap. She approached the boys and squinted at them. It took a second before she recognized Rudy and Alex.

"Oh, yeah," she said, snapping her fingers. She looked down at her coffee can of cracked walnuts. "You hungry?"

"No, not really," Rudy said. He pulled his sloshing bucket up to her and asked with a grin, "You wanna buy a fish?"

"What?" she said, nosing the surface of the water. "*¿Qué es esto?* What is this? It looks like a dirty rag."

"No, Mrs. Estrada," Alex said. "It's Fishsticks. Rudy caught him over at Minkler."

"Yeah, Mrs. Estrada," Rudy butted in. "I thought you might like to buy him."

"I already got a fish—Buster." She poked a finger at the fish, breaking the surface of the water. "Boy, oh boy, he's a biggie."

"Yeah, he sure is, and Buster is probably lonely. Fishes should go in pairs, like socks and shoes."

"Like *tortillas y frijoles*," Alex added.

Mrs. Estrada took the bucket from Rudy and asked them to follow her.

When they entered the house, they were greeted by a herd of unruly kittens, all meowing and jumping at the boys' legs. Rudy shook one from his leg and one from his shoe. They followed Mrs. Estrada to her bedroom, where she flicked on the overhead light and greeted her fish in the aquarium, "Buster, you have a friend."

Mrs. Estrada tapped the glass with a knuckle. Buster sent up a huge bubble, as if he were listening to Mrs. Estrada.

Rudy and Alex dropped to their knees and stared at Buster, who stared back at them.

"Buster better make room for Fishstick," Rudy said.

"How much you want for your fish?" Mrs. Estrada asked, getting down to business.

"How about ten dollars?"

"Ten dollars!" she screamed. "Shoot, for that price, I could defrost one of the trouts in the freezer and let Buster play with him."

"How 'bout eight," Alex said. "Buster looks pretty lonely to me." He raised the bucket for Buster to see his new friend. "See how excited he is?"

Buster was now flapping his tail and fins and sending up a blast of bubbles.

"Hmmm, you're right," Mrs. Estrada agreed. "How 'bout seven bucks plus some cookies."

"Sold," Rudy said.

To lower the water level, Mrs. Estrada scooped some of it from the aquarium. She carefully raised Fishstick into her cupped plams and let the fish slide into its new home. Buster sent up more bubbles and flapped his fins. The two fish stared at each other, right eye for Buster and left eye for Fishstick. They worked their gills and fins and in their cramped aquarium swam in place without getting anywhere.

Chapter **8**

Rudy and Alex huddled together in the kitchen, mulling over their new job: handwriting analysis. Rudy had come up with this scheme when his mother handed him a grocery list. He noted that her handwriting sloped left. The letters almost seemed to fall over. He knew it meant something—either she was driven to succeed or was just so plain tired that she was ready to collapse. He had bought the eggs and milk and on the way home noticed the graffiti-splattered walls, the handwriting of *vatos locos*, gang members.

Some of the graffiti belonged to Slinky. His *placa* was *SR* squared off in a giant fist and was pretty easy to analyze. *SR* meant Slinky Rodriguez, and it meant trouble.

After these first observations, Rudy imagined he could invite his sister's friends over to analyze their boyfriends' handwriting. He was going to charge them fifty cents a read, a fair deal since they spent a hundred times that much when it came to clothes and eyeliner.

"Man, you don't know anything about that handwriting stuff," laughed Estela. She leaned on the stove as a batch of popcorn was ticking time on the back burner. Rudy continued his sales pitch and followed his sister into the living room. Estela had just broken up with her boyfriend but was considering getting back together with him if he bought her some earrings she had seen at K-mart.

Rudy tried to persuade Estela by appealing to her curiosity about the supernatural. He told her his strange dreams about riding the backs of dolphins and how he could smell through his ears. Once when a water balloon was ready to hit him from behind, a cosmic eye had opened up on the back of his head. He said, straight-faced, that he moved a glass of water just by looking at it. Estela only laughed. "Dude, you're really weird."

Rudy had to laugh himself, knowing he sounded weird. He said, "Give it a try, *ruca*. Get your girls over here. You'll find out more about your boyfriends from me than any of your bathroom gossip."

In the end, thinking that it might be fun, Estela called three of her best friends. They arrived, sneering at Rudy and Alex. They immediately headed to the bathroom, where they teased their hair and pouted in the mirror. They looked *bad*.

Now Rudy and Alex sat in the kitchen, worried.

"You sure you can talk that trash?" Alex said.

"I think I can," Rudy said. He was nervous because his sister had invited Brenda Lopez, one really tough cookie. She could take the monkey bars in threes, hit homers like the boys, kick the bad air from kickballs, and suck a Big Gulp in less than an Olympic-timed minute. It was reported that her palm slap could rip a tetherball from its chain and send it up to the roof of the school.

The girls, all seventh graders, came out of

the bathroom, snapping watermelon bubble gum. They reeked of perfume. Their narrow eyes were hatchet-shaped, with mascara and black lining all around.

"Okay, man," Rachel smirked. "Tell us about our boyfriends. Is their love true or false?" She waved a letter at Rudy, and the other girls waved theirs as well.

"It's fifty cents a read," Rudy said flatly.

"Look at him, girls." Rachel laughed. "He thinks he's a businessman."

"He *is* a busy person," Alex said. He felt suddenly brave, though he knew any one of them could stomp him into the ground.

"Who are you, *gordo*?" Brenda asked. Her hatchet eyebrows went down.

"I'm his business partner."

The four girls laughed. Brenda clicked her tongue and remarked, "You trying to talk like a *gavacho*? I saw you guys collecting soda cans."

Still, the girls followed them into the kitchen. Rachel handed Rudy her letter from Larry Delgado, a high school freshman. Rudy read the letter to himself, lips moving. The letter read:

Baby, I'm sorry that you feel like I don't like you. But I like you lots. Remember that soda we shared. That was good, huh? Baby, I think of you all the time I'm at school. That's why I don't know my algebra. I can't study, homegirl. I'm stuck on you, like *frijoles y tortillas*. . . .

Rudy read the letter. He laid it down, looked at Rachel, and jabbered without much thought, "He's a fox."

"Sure, he's good-looking," Rachel said.

"No, I mean, he's—" Rudy started to say something, then stopped. He was going to report that Larry was as sneaky as a fox, not good-looking. But he realized if he said anything bad, she would report it back to her boyfriend, and Larry would hunt him down. Rudy gulped and said instead, "He's clever. He's . . . kisses really good, huh?"

The girls laughed.

"He dances good."

The girls laughed and danced.

"He's strong."

The girls curled up their arms, making muscles.

"He's tough."

"*Pues*, I saw him throw some *chingadazos* with some bad dudes," Rachel admitted, out of breath from dancing. Her bubble gum flopped around in her mouth when she laughed and clapped her hands. *"Dime."*

"He's going to be a success."

"¿Cómo?"

Rudy studied the letter again and stared at the sloppy penmanship. After a quiet moment, he raised his gaze up to Rachel. "He's going into the army and gonna be a hero."

"¡Chale! He says he's going to the Marines."

The girls laughed and danced until their mascara began to bleed black from their eyes. They returned to the bathroom, where they redid their faces and loaded up on more perfume.

"Man, Rudy, that was close." Alex groaned.

"Yeah, I'm scared." He pocketed the five sweaty dimes that Rachel tossed at him.

"You better be cool. I don't think they like us. You don't think Estela will let them beat us up?"

"Nah. She's my sister, ain't she?"

"That's why. Just be cool."

When they returned, Brenda squeezed the

back of Rudy's neck and said, "Tell me some lies, homeboy. Marta, you go next."

Rudy knew Marta from school. A real brainhead, Marta was sharp as a knife in a fried *papa*. She had been put ahead two grades and was the geography champ of the whole city. Rudy knew that she knew all about math and English, but when he unfolded the letter, Rudy knew she didn't know about boys. The love letter was from Slinky!

"*¡Ay, Dios!*" Rudy shouted. He flapped the letter at Alex, whose eyes got big when he saw Slinky's *placa* at the bottom of the letter.

"You know this homeboy?" Marta asked.

"Just a little bit," Rudy answered. Sweat began to slide down his oily nose. "I used to see him at the playground."

"Little bit ain't nothin'," Marta said. "For fifty cents you better tell me something valuable. I think he's a skunk!"

Rudy didn't say anything to this. He gazed over Slinky's misspelled words. It was a letter telling Marta why he hadn't shown up at the theater. It was an apology. He said that someone stole his bike and that he found it without wheels on a ditch bank.

"*Pues.* Get your *boca* goin'!" Marta snapped.

"Can I have some water?" Rudy whined.

"No," Estela said. "Lick your lips and start saying something."

"Slinky . . . he likes you a lot, Marta," Rudy started feebly. "But he's kind of afraid of—"

"He ain't afraid of nobody. You callin' him a scaredy cat?" Marta said, fists doubled.

"No, no," Rudy corrected. "Let me finish. I'm saying that he's afraid to say how much you mean to him because, you know, he's the kind of guy who don't know how to be romantic."

Marta liked this. Brenda, Rachel, and Estela liked this. They seemed to be pleased as they chewed and snapped their bubble gum.

Rudy squirmed some more praise for Slinky and then added as a final note, "He's committed to you for the rest of the summer."

"That's all I want him for. I gotta be sure that he'll take me to the dance."

Brenda then flapped her letter in Rudy's face.

"Okay, my turn," Brenda said, smoothing Rudy's ducktailed hair. "Make it sweet."

Rudy took the letter, which was from her ex-boyfriend "Porky" Cruz. The letter started with pledges of commitment to her and the Los Angeles Raiders. He told her he liked her because she was for real, and that if they ever got mad at each other, they would understand and kiss and make up.

"*Mentiroso*," she snapped. "He's nothing but a cheat. I saw him with that *ruca* from Sanger. *Una flaquita.* I'll scratch her eyes out if I see her in Fresno."

The girls laughed and waited for Rudy to interpret the letter.

"Okay, man," Brenda said, squeezing his neck. "Say something, homey."

"He's, he's—" Rudy started. "He's got a nice personality."

"Yeah?"

"He's got *corazón*."

"Yeah?"

"He's wild for you, but he don't know how to show his true feelings."

"*Pues*, that might be true," Brenda said, looking at Estela, eyes big and the hatchets of her penciled eyebrows going up and down, ready to strike. "*¿Qué más, chavalito?*"

"I think the way his letters are so tall, he

. . . kinda likes to walk tall in life. He don't take nothing from nobody. And I can tell positively that he's in love with you from the way he crosses his T's."

"You know all this from his handwriting?" Brenda asked, releasing her hand from the back of Rudy's neck. She winked at Rachel. She nodded her head at Estela and Marta. She turned her head and spat her now tasteless gum into the sink. It plopped into a cereal bowl.

"Sure he does," Alex interrupted. "Rudy's got a special gift to read handwriting."

"*Y tú,*" Brenda asked. "You got a special gift?"

"No. I'm just an ordinary human being."

The four girls laughed.

"Look at the human bean," Brenda smirked. Then suddenly Brenda's smile collapsed, and her eyes grew wild. "*Sabes,* homeboy, this is not a letter to me. It's to a girl he was messin' with when I caught him *como un ratón.*"

Rudy was caught, not unlike *un ratón.* He started to stand up and was shoved back down —hard.

"I just need a drink of water," Rudy explained. He looked over at the sink, where the water plopped onto the morning dishes.

"Lick your lips, like your big sister tol' you," Brenda snapped.

"I was just gettin ready to say that you better watch out because his writing shows he has a tendency to be a two-timer," Rudy faltered.

"You don't know nothing," an upset Rachel said. "Give me back my money."

Rudy pulled the five dimes from his pocket. He tried to smile and explain that it was all for fun. He tried to tell them that he had read a book about handwriting and remembered what sloping handwriting meant. Not everything he said was untrue. The girls told him to shut up. They pushed Rudy and Alex to the living room. The girls huddled together, whispering, laughing, and throwing mean looks at the boys, who sat on the edge of the couch, scared.

"For punishment—" Estela started to say.

"For punishment," Brenda interrupted, "you got to write five hundred times, 'I will not lie 'bout love letters or play with women's hearts.'"

"That's not fair," Alex whined.

"Shut up, *gordo*," Brenda scolded. "For you, six hundred times. We're going out for some sodas. When we come back, you better be sailing across the pages."

"What if we refuse?" Rudy asked.

"Are you serious?" Rachel glared.

"We'll throw you outside in your *chones* if you don't do it," Marta answered.

The girls left and took with them the reek of perfume.

Rudy and Alex had no choice but to lick their lips and then their pencils. They started looping words across unlined papers, all the while trying to figure out where they went wrong.

Chapter 9

"You mean you're not mad at me?" Rudy asked in astonishment. Slinky had called on the telephone. It was Saturday morning, breakfast, and Rudy had just swallowed *chorizo con huevos* pinched up in a tortilla. He cleared his throat and asked a second time, "You sure you're not going to kill me?"

"No, man," Slinky said. "The Discman didn't belong to me. I borrowed it from Trucha Mendoza. I tried to tell you at the wedding."

Rudy nearly dropped the phone when he

heard Trucha's name. While Slinky was a playground *vato loco*, Trucha was an honest-to-goodness gangster with a self-cut tattoo on his right fist. The tattoo spelled "H O M E Y," and lucky for Rudy, he had never seen the letters up close.

"Man, I'm good as dead!" Rudy cried. "Did you tell Trucha?"

"*Chale.*"

"What are we gonna do?"

"Don't worry. We still got a couple of days. He's with *su familia* in L.A. On vacation."

"Are you really telling me the truth? You're not trying to trick me," Rudy asked, not quite convinced, even though Slinky's voice was steady.

"Listen, man, this ain't April Fool's. This is serious."

"How serious?"

"We can't play around, Rudy," Slinky said. "We got to figure a way to get some money. I'm telling you the truth."

Slinky suggested that they meet later to come up with a plan of action. They decided to meet at the monkey bars at Holmes Playground. Rudy returned to his breakfast, his appetite destroyed. He forced himself to eat, though, because he knew it was going to be a long day. After he took his plate to the sink, he asked for advice from his father, who was in the living room, his feet up on the hassock. He was reading the newspaper.

"Dad," Rudy asked as he plopped on the couch. "You ever get in any trouble when you were little?"

"Trouble?" his father teased. He ran his fingers down his chin, pulling on an invisible beard. He became reflective. He shook his head and answered, "Nah, I don't think so. I was a saint."

"Dad, come on. Level with me," Rudy pleaded.

His dad put down his newspaper and told Rudy that he had gotten into more trouble than a fox in a chicken coop. He had played with matches, gotten in fights, jumped from rooftops, squirted his grandfather with a hose, chased girls with a *moco* on his finger, eaten crayons and paste, burped in church, and stolen fruit from trees—all by the time he was six years old! Hearing this litany of bad behavior, Rudy felt better. His problem seemed like a piece of cake—sweet and easy.

"So what's going on with you?" his father asked. "You in trouble?"

Rudy hesitated, two fingers in his mouth. He wasn't sure how much he should tell his father. He might get yelled at, but he told him the truth. "Well, I broke this guy's Discman."

Rudy explained his problem, and how he and Alex had been looking for work to pay for the Discman. He described Slinky as big as King Kong and just as mean. His father listened until his son finished. "Sounds like tough luck, Rudy." He stood up and brought out three dollars from his wallet. "This might help."

"Dad, you're teasing me," Rudy said.

"*¡Chale!* Take it," his father said, thrusting the money at Rudy like a bouquet of flowers.

"Thanks, Dad," Rudy said, and stuffed the money into his front pocket. He knew that he would need every bit. He knew his father was a good guy.

His father smiled. "Okay, Rudy, get to work. You broke it, you replace it."

Rudy got up from the couch and called Alex.

The two met at a 7-Eleven store, where Rudy treated Alex to a soda and sunflower seeds. Then they started off toward Holmes Playground. Rudy carried a large paper bag. He was hoping to find some aluminum cans on the way. With the sale of Fishstick and with his earnings from baby-sitting and playing in his uncle's group, he now had twenty-seven dollars and thirty-five cents. He kept his money stuffed in a gym sock in his drawer.

"You sure Slinky's on the level?" Alex asked.

"*Simón*," Rudy answered. He spotted a soda can and raced toward it, screaming as he jumped high into the air. The weight of his stomp sent a squirt of orange soda into the air. Rudy bagged the can, and they continued on to the playground.

Slinky wasn't at the monkey bars but at the swings. He was pushing a screaming little kid.

"Here goes," Rudy said, swallowing a lump of saliva and fear.

The two of them slowly approached Slinky, a seventh grader who was a foot taller than them. His face was as long as a banana and just as yellow. When Slinky raised his hand to wave, Rudy and Alex cowered. They thought Slinky was getting ready to slap them.

"Nah, man, I ain't mad," Slinky said, and then pointed at the paper bag.

"Is that your brother?" Rudy asked. The kid on the swing had tears running from his eyes. He jumped off the swing and began to run away.

"Nah, he's just a punk," Slinky answered. "What you got there?"

"A soda can."

"You mean you drank the soda and didn't leave any for me?"

"Nah, collecting them," Alex explained. He wasn't going to mention the soda that he and Rudy just sloshed down.

"When does Trucha come back?" Rudy asked.

"Wednesday."

"We only got four days."

"Rudy's been working," Alex butted in. "I've been helping him."

Rudy then explained his jobs, from roofing a doghouse to pulling fish from a river.

"So what's left?" Slinky asked. With a match, he was cleaning the moons of dirt from his fingernails.

"I don't know," Rudy said. "How about picking grapes?"

"You mean, like, real work?" Slinky asked, his face sour.

"Slinky's right," Alex said. "We got to find an easy job."

"Washing cars?" Rudy asked.

"No."

"Weeding a flower bed?"

"No."

"Hauling trash?"

"No."

Alex snapped his fingers and said, "I got it. A chain letter! We write people we know and ask for money."

Rudy's face brightened, but Slinky's face screwed up, as if in pain.

"You don't think it's a good idea?" Rudy asked.

"Yeah, it's pretty good," Slinky said, definitely in pain. "I got this stupid match stuck up my fingernail!" He showed Rudy and Alex the tear of blood that began to leak from under his fingernail. He sucked his finger as they sprinted to Rudy's house.

When they got there, no one was home. Rudy was hoping to tell his father that everything was okay—sort of. Instead they got down to work. Rudy typed on the antique computer: "Save the ozone! Send this letter to five friends."

"What's this 'bout the ozone?" Slinky asked.

"People won't have to smell us getting slaughtered by Trucha."

"Seems pretty good to me," Alex said, nodding his head.

"Print it out," Slinky told Rudy. "Go for it."

They then went through Rudy's mother's address books and wrote out envelopes. But there was an expense: twenty first-class stamps, which they bought at the drugstore. Still, Rudy figured that all their lives were worth the five dollars for stamps. He figured they were worth at least eight dollars. The three of the them licked the stamps and hurried to the post office.

"Okay, *¿qué más?*" said Rudy as he watched the letters slide down the chute of the mailbox. "We need to do something."

"Like what?" Slinky whined. "I thought we just did something."

"We need to get another job," Rudy said.

"It'll take at least a couple of days before money rolls in."

The three of them crossed the street. Rudy spotted the glimmer of two soda cans. He stomped the last dribbles of soda from them and kicked them into his bag.

They returned to the playground and sat in the bleachers, their chins propped in the palms of their hands. They thought until their heads hurt, but they only came up with boring jobs that would raise blisters on their palms and make them sweaty. Rudy told them about the reward for the lost cat, but they waved off that suggestion and said he was *loco*.

"That cat is probably road kill," Slinky sneered. "Like us if we don't get some more money."

"Wait a minute," Alex said. "I got it."

"What?" Slinky asked.

"Air guitar." He sighed happily, his eyes locked on the horizon of salvation.

"No way," Slinky said.

"Yeah, man, I seen it done in front of Disneyland." Alex stood up and pretended to play a guitar, his body dancing and a scowl cutting dark shadows on his face.

Rudy looked at Slinky, and Slinky shrugged his shoulders and asked, "Okay, what's the plan?"

Alex stopped playing air guitar. He told them that they could get his brother's cassette player, find a corner at the mall, and scream their fool heads off. They would play guitar to the music and collect coins and stinky dollar bills from onlookers. They hurried to Alex's house, where they made themselves peanut butter tortillas and drank a pitcher of lime-flavored Kool-Aid.

"Slinky," Rudy confessed. "I was always scared of you."

"Me," Slinky said, as if surprised. "Nah, I'm a kitten." He hugged Rudy kind of hard and playfully slapped Alex's back. A spurt of Kool-Aid jumped from Alex's nostrils. Alex coughed and yelled, "Slinky, you don't know your own strength."

"Listen, dudes. I wanted to mess you up, but I need your help. ¿*Entiendes*, Mendez?"

Rudy and Alex nodded their heads. Then they made a crude sign using cardboard and crayons. The sign read: AIR BROTHERS DE FRESNO.

When Alex saw his mother pull into the driveway, her hair piled with blue and yellow curlers, he said, "Let's split. I know my mom is gonna put me to work."

Alex grabbed his brother's cassette player and pocketed a few tapes. With Slinky leading the way, they ran out the back door and up the alley. They kicked along, quiet in the afternoon sun, and pulled a few apricots hanging over a fence. Rudy stuffed his face until it was sticky.

The boys arrived at the mall and stood by Penny's, unsure how to start. Shoppers were dragging their bags around. All of them looked as hot and red as lobsters in boiling water.

"Who's gonna play first?" Slinky asked.

"How about you," Alex said.

"*Chale*, homes." He looked at Rudy and said, "Dude, you go first."

Rudy was scared that Slinky would hug him hard a second time, so he sighed and said, "Okay."

A couple stopped to see what the three boys were up to. Some kids on skateboards cruised over, along with two others on bicycles. Then a woman with two babies in her arms stopped to watch the commotion. Suddenly there was a crowd as Rudy took a dramatically sweeping bow.

"We're the Air Brothers," Rudy sang, his leg jerking to a rhythm inside his bobbing head. "We come from Fresno, and our hearts *son puros mexicanos. ¡Órale!*"

Rudy nodded at Alex, who pushed a tape into the cassette. Legs splayed and mean-looking, Rudy got ready. He fingered his invisible guitar. He shook his head as if his hair were in his way. But when the music blared, it wasn't rap, heavy metal, or oldies but goodies. It wasn't rock or even Mexican music. It was Hawaiian music and the watery twang of a ukulele.

"Hey, Alex!" Rudy screamed as he strummed his air guitar. "You got the wrong music!"

"Keep playing!" Alex shouted. "I think it's my mom's tape. I'll fix it." He dropped onto his knees and squinted at the tape in the window of the cassette. The hand-scrawled label said, WORLD MUSIC.

A nervous Rudy smiled a toothy smile at the audience and played air guitar. He strummed and strummed and even sang, "Aloha oe, you silvery sea . . ." He sang with all his Hawaiian heart, and then strummed and danced to Russian music, his arms across his chest as he shouted, "Hey, hey, hey." He danced a Polish polka with Slinky as his partner. He stomped an Argentinian cowboy two-step. And in the end, the three were pint-size mariachis, each strumming the air guitar of love ballads. They crowed, *"Sabor a mí,"* and brought tears to the eyes of at least two elderly women.

The crowd showered Rudy with applause and the tinkle of dimes and nickels and a silver dollar from Mrs. Estrada, clutching a shopping bag and a box of popcorn. She shouted, "Hey, *chamacos,* my cats got fleas again! Come over if you boys need real work."

Chapter **10**

Rudy, Alex, and Slinky didn't bother to go to Mrs. Estrada's house. Instead, they sat in the shade of a mulberry tree, letting their fingers swim through the coins and crumpled bills. They had never felt so rich. They had pocketed almost sixteen dollars just by learning how to dance Hawaiian.

"Man, we should go into show biz," Slinky commented as he flipped a coin and smacked it against his wrist. Without looking, he called, "Heads."

Rudy and Alex nodded. To keep on his good

side, they agreed anytime Slinky spoke, even though the coin was really tails.

Rudy recounted the money and then added the money he had at home—sixty-four dollars, plus the crushed alumium cans in the paper bag. They were still about forty dollars short. He figured they needed another job.

"I got to go, dudes," Slinky said, rising to his feet. "I got a date with Linda Ruiz."

"I thought she was Trucha's girl?" Rudy asked.

"So? She's my girl until he comes back." Slinky stretched his hardened arms skyward and then swiftly ripped two dollars from Rudy's hands. "I got to buy her a soda. Rudy, you *piojito*, hang on to the money and cans. You better not think 'bout leaving town!" He laughed and walked away, his long legs scissoring the hot air of a Saturday afternoon.

"He's asking for it." Rudy sighed. He wondered how long Slinky would stay alive.

"Yeah," Alex agreed. "If Trucha finds out, he's road kill for sure."

Rudy clicked his fingers and then said, "I got an easy idea! Let's sell flowers."

"Homes, we ain't got any flowers."

"My grandma Martha does. She's in Mexico

visiting her sister. She won't know the differ-
ence if we cut some."

Rudy had always noticed people standing at
busy corners selling flowers. He spied their
buckets of roses and carnations and saw that
the vendors sat under umbrellas, sucking on
sodas while listening to the radio. To him, it
looked easy, not like washing cars or mowing
lawns.

"Let's go, homes," Rudy said while he rose
to his feet and brushed grass off his pants.

They scampered up the street, the metallic
clap of grimy quarters, dimes, and nickels in
their pockets.

Rudy's grandmother's rickety house was
bright with flowers. They stood in coffee cans
on the porch, wooden boxes in front of the
garage, and along the fence in the backyard.
Flowers even blossomed on the roof, where
the wind had sent seeds and enough dirt for
flowers to scratch out a life.

"You think it's okay to take some?" Alex
asked. "I don't want to get in trouble."

"Sure. Grandma is pretty cool. If she knew I
was in this trouble, she'd scold me first and
then lend me the money."

The boys clipped bunches of red and yellow

roses and placed them in a bucket. Rudy pressed his nose into one, sniffed hard, and sneezed. The head of the rose blew off, scattering the petals.

"They smell good," Rudy said as he pinched a string of *mocos*—snot—from the end of his nose.

"*¡Asco!*" Alex yelled. "You got some on my shoes."

"Sorry, homes."

They took an armful of newspaper for wrapping the best flowers. With water sloshing from the bucket, they hurried up the street toward a busy intersection. By the time they got there, they were hot and sweaty and realized they didn't have an umbrella for protection from the sun. They huddled in the shade of a billboard. When the first wave of cars stopped at the red light, they shouted, "Flowers! Fresh flowers from Grandma's house!"

The drivers and passengers just looked at the boys, and a poodle yapped his crooked teeth at them. The cars sped away, coloring the air with black exhaust. Another wave of cars approached, and again they yelled, "Flowers. Fresh-cut flowers!" Again the drivers and passengers just looked at the boys and sped away.

"This is sorry," Rudy cried.

"It ain't that bad," Alex tried to comfort him. "At least nobody's bothering us."

But he spoke too soon. A kid in the back of a pickup flicked a bottle cap at them. He missed by a mile, but Alex and Rudy were ready to hurl their bodies at this boy, they were so mad. But the truck took off, jerking forward as the kid smirked at them.

They sold one bunch of flowers to a woman who talked and talked. Rudy and Alex learned so much about her family that they believed any minute she would invite them home for dinner. Still, it was a fifty-cent sale, and they kept smiling through the singsong yakking about her sixteen cousins from Michoacán.

They screamed "Fresh flowers!" for an hour, their faces burning from the heat and collecting the grit of a dusty street corner.

"This is a sorry job," Rudy muttered.

"Really sorry," Alex agreed. He wiped his T-shirt over his sweaty face and said, "Let's get a soda."

"We can't spend our money, homes. It's for the Discman."

Rudy licked his dry lips and responded, "Yeah, you're right."

An ice cream cart wobbled up the street. The hatted man jiggled a bell on his cart and yelled, "*¡Helados! ¡Helados de banana, coco, manzana, naranja, fresa!*"

Rudy tugged on Alex's T-shirt, and leaning his head toward Alex's, he whispered, "Watch this. I'll show you how cool I can be."

"*Señor*, let's make a trade," Rudy said politely in Spanish as the man approached them. "Some flowers for two ice creams."

The man stopped his cart. He sized Rudy and Alex up, unsure of what they were up to. He sniffed the flowers and brought a wilting rose up from the bucket. He examined the rose and placed it back in the bucket, when a petal dropped.

"Your flowers are almost dead," he finally concluded. "I'll give you some ice."

"Ice?" Rudy shouted.

"Why, yes. These roses are ready for the grave."

"What do you mean? We just picked them."

The man shook his head and smiled. His gold teeth gleamed in the summer light. He brought out a smashed ice cream drumstick and a handful of chipped ice.

They made the trade. The man got three bunches of flowers, and the boys got one smashed ice cream and six slivers of bluish ice. He maneuvered his cart up the street, yelling *"¡Helados! ¡Helados! ¡Helados y rosas bonitas!"* He turned and winked at the boys, who sat on the curb.

"Man, I think we got taken again!" Alex cried.

They sucked on the ice and shared the ice cream, lapping up its sweetness by turns.

"What's the worst thing you ever did?" Rudy asked, licking his fingers. He was bored as a *burro* tied to a post.

"When I was six, I told my cousin Lupe that peanut butter was like leather polish, so he put some on his shoes."

"No way."

"De veras." Alex laughed. "He smelled like a sandwich for days." He laughed until he coughed and his eyes watered. "What did you do?"

Rudy thought about it, finger on his chin. He was good most days, but he had moments when devil horns seemed to grow from his forehead. "When I was real little, I pulled the arms from my G.I. Joes and flushed them down the toilet." He laughed as he remembered waving good-bye to the arms as they swirled in the toilet water. He sighed and looked at the remaining bunch of roses in their bucket. He was bending over to sniff their perfume when he heard, "Rudy! Alex! You *piojitos.*"

They squinted in the harsh sunlight before they recognized Slinky cruising on his bike. Linda Ruiz was giggling on the handlebars. Slinky came to a skidding halt, scattering Rudy and Alex, who kicked over the bucket of roses.

"Ooops!" Slinky sang.

"Ah, Slinky," Alex moaned, his hands flopping at his side, "look at what you did."

"Accidents happen, homeboys," Slinky said, ignoring Alex's complaint. He let a mouthful of sunflower seed shells blow from his mouth. One landed on Alex's arm. Alex slapped it off and made a face at Slinky.

"We're selling flowers," Rudy said, straightening the bucket.

"Any luck, homeboys?" He tossed another handful of seeds into his mouth.

Rudy looked at Alex, and Alex looked at Rudy, not answering.

Slinky turned his attention to the remaining bunch of roses and said, "Babe, I'll show you what love is!" He clicked his fingers at Rudy, who knew better than to complain. He grabbed the roses, pricking himself, and wrapped them in newspaper. He handed them to Slinky, who handed them to Linda. She blushed the color of the roses and gave Slinky a peck on his cheek, which was stuffed with half-churned sunflower seeds. She sniffed the roses and sneezed. They sped away, the roses scenting the air with gossip that Trucha would certainly discover.

Rudy looked at the bucket and said, "Let's get out of here, Alex."

"You mean, out of town?"

"Nah, just home."

The two started walking home, dejected. They knew that Trucha would find out everything.

Rudy could see his life flash under the hammer blows of Trucha's fists. His lip would grow fat as a water balloon from an uppercut, and air would gush from his belly. He would taste blood flowing freely from his nose. But

he was no dummy. He decided that he should hit up his father for money and pay it back when he could.

But these images of destruction disappeared when right in front of them he saw their salvation: the orange cat with a white mustache. Dollar signs rang up in Rudy's eyes.

"Alex, it's Pudding," Rudy whispered.

"Whatta you, *loco*? That's a cat," Alex snarled. "You been in the sun too long."

"I know I been in the sun too long, but it's that cat with the reward."

Rudy and Alex stared at the cat, who was licking a front paw. Pudding stopped, meowed, and walked right into Rudy's outstretched arms.

Chapter **11**

Rudy and Alex hurried home to call the woman for the reward. As they jogged in flapping tennis shoes, they beamed at Pudding, their furry salvation, nestled in Rudy's arms. Pudding's head bounced with each stride.

Breathing hard, with fingers of sweat choking their necks, the boys ran into Rudy's room and searched for the lost cat flyer among the piles of dirty clothes and comic books. They found it on the dresser shaped into a paper airplane. Rudy unfolded the flyer and stared at the telephone number: 555-4718.

"You're saved, *ese*," Alex said.

The two boys hurried to the kitchen, where they first drank ice water and then called for the reward.

"Come on," Rudy pleaded. "Answer!" The telephone rang thirteen times before he slowly hung up. "She's not home."

The boys lowered their heads, dejected, and returned to the living room, where they found Pudding struggling halfway up the curtains.

When Rudy shouted, "Get down, Pudding," and clapped his hands, the cat turned, glared, and hissed at Rudy. He pulled him from the curtain and scolded him.

They took the cat to the front lawn and fed him a bowl of aging tuna salad from the refrigerator. They stuck a glob of tuna on the end of their fingers and let the cat lick it off.

"That sixty-five dollars will save our lives," Alex remarked.

The next day they called again, but still there was no answer. Pudding was nothing but trouble. He kicked over an open can of motor oil in the garage, jumped onto the kitchen table and licked bologna, brought in a half-eaten sparrow, and bit Rudy's mother's finger when she tried to pet him. After that, his mother said the cat had to go.

They called on the third day, and still there was no answer. The telephone rang and rang.

"Man, this is sorry," Rudy said as he lowered the telephone and, turning around, found Pudding with his head in a bag of ranch-flavored potato chips. "Pudding! You're bad!"

"Let's go outside," Alex suggested.

The boys threw themselves on the front lawn and played with Pudding, teasing him with a branch.

Slinky arrived on his bicycle, cutting a black skid mark on the sidewalk. He hopped off and admired his bicycle *placa*.

"Trucha's coming home tomorrow, homeboys," Slinky said as he sat on the grass and playfully boxed Pudding, who took a swipe at Slinky and hissed. He turned to Rudy. "How much you got, man?"

Rudy pulled out wads of bills and coins and after counting the pile twice, mumbled, "Seventy-three dollars."

"We need more," Slinky said, now worried. He was chewing a stalk of grass with vigor. "Trucha's bad news."

"It'll be worse when Trucha finds out you gave Linda a ride on your bike," Rudy stated.

"They broke up," he said. "She's as free as a bird. She can do what she wants."

Two sparrows began to bicker in the trees, which made Pudding lift his face skyward. Two fangs glistened, and his whiskers twitched.

"Funny-looking cat." Slinky laughed. "I like the dude's *bigote*, that little mustache. You sure we can get sixty-five dollars for the *vato gato*?"

"*Simón.*"

From his pants pocket, Rudy pulled the reward flyer, wrinkled as a shirt, and tossed it at Slinky. He read it and then looked at Pudding. "Who would think he's worth anything? I just hope we can get our hands on *el dinero* before Trucha returns. That Discman was top of the line."

"I said I'm sorry I smashed it," Rudy said. He pulled up a tuft of grass and tossed it at Pudding, who was asleep, his eyes squeezed softly together.

"Homeboy, you run wild at baseball. Next time, stay in the lines and don't trip."

"Yeah." Rudy sighed.

The three boys lay on the lawn, eyes closed and sleepy from the summer heat. Rudy thought of the ocean. He would love to throw himself, head first, into the white lip of an oncoming wave. He would love to buckle up in a parachute, as his older cousin had done in Mazatlán, and have a speedboat pull him along the coast like a human kite.

But he woke from this summer slumber when he heard skid marks eating up the sidewalk. He sat up and nearly collapsed again, because in front of him was Trucha, the big fish of the *barrio*. He was dressed in khakis and a white T-shirt. His hair was black as polished shoes.

Trucha spat out a mouthful of sunflower seeds and slurred, *"Qué pasa,* homeboys."

Slinky sat up with flakes of grass clinging to his hair. He was scared. He swallowed hard, grinned at Trucha, and said, "Good to see you, homes. I thought you were coming home tomorrow."

"You thought wrong, Slinky."

"How was Disneyland? You go on the teacups?" Slinky tried to sound cheerful.

"Forget the teacups!" Trucha growled. "I let you borrow my main piece. Cough it up, homes." His eyes were thin slits. For a split second Rudy thought he could slip nickels in them and turn his nose like a knob, just like a parking meter.

"Oh, yeah, I think we—" Slinky started to say.

"Don't think, homes. Just hand it over! *¿Sabes?*" Trucha had gotten off his bike and was now staring holes through Slinky.

"Trucha," Rudy volunteered after he swallowed and cleared his throat of fear, "I broke it."

"*¿Qué?*"

"I was playing baseball, and we were playing against guys from Tulare Street."

Rudy explained how he rounded third, tripped, and landed on a pile of clothes and gear. Trucha listened, his face flat without emotion. Rudy couldn't tell whether he was really angry or just upset.

"But it was really my fault," Slinky squeaked, hands gesturing to himself. "I shouldn't have lent it to my stupid brother."

"*¿Qué pasó?* What is this, confession time?" Trucha asked, circling the three. "You altar boys?"

Rudy could now see that he was mad, but

not so mad that he was going to tie them into knots. This could happen later, but for now they seemed on safe ground.

"But we're going to pay you back," Alex said.

Trucha glared at Alex. "Who are you, *gordo*? Their accountant?"

"In a way, so to speak."

"You getting smart with me, *ese*?" Trucha took a step toward Alex, spitting sunflower seeds, both hands curled into fists.

"We got the money, Trucha," Rudy said, stepping between Alex and Trucha. *"En serio."*

When he pulled out the wad of bills and coins, Trucha's eyes got big momentarily, then narrowed back to slits. He pocketed the money without any of them saying a word.

"Yeah," Rudy continued. "It's seventy-two dollars and some change, and we're getting a reward for Pudding."

"Who's Pudding?" Trucha asked. "Never heard of the dude. Is he a *vato loco* from the *barrio*?"

"Chale, he's a *vato gato*!" Rudy said. "His name is Pudding, but he's called Principe, Bud, and—"

At this roll of names, Pudding woke, stretched, and rose to his four paws. He meowed and twitched his ears until grass shook off.

"The dude's worth sixty-five dollars, Trucha," Alex explained.

Trucha glared at Alex and hissed, "What are you, a banker? How do you know so much?"

"The cat is lost," Rudy explained. "There's a reward."

"It's true! Scout's honor!" Slinky said, fingers up like rabbit ears. "Show our *carnal* the reward flyer."

Rudy unfolded the flyer and handed it to Trucha, who crumpled it into a ball and threw it on the lawn. Rudy picked it up and stuffed it into his pocket.

As Trucha glared and churned a mouthful of sunflower seeds, Rudy apologized for breaking the Discman and said that for more than a week he had been doing odd jobs. He told Trucha how he and his pal Alex had combed cats, roofed a doghouse, sold a door and bought it back at a loss, played in a mariachi band, caught fish, and sold apricots and flowers. He was explaining how he was even collecting soda cans when Trucha snapped,

"Shut up, *sapo*," as he gently picked up Pudding. "This *gato* is worth sixty-five dollars?"

"Yeah," all three sang like choirboys.

"How come you don't cash him in, then?" Trucha asked.

"The owner's not home."

Trucha eyed the three boys and then sneered, "*Mira*, we're going to get our reward. If that owner don't pay up, you *vatos* are gonna hate life."

"But we like life," Rudy said lightly.

"Me too," Alex said.

"You guys better be telling the truth," Trucha warned. "You better not be playing with me."

"They are telling the truth!" Slinky said.

"Shut up, man."

Trucha petted Pudding softly, and Pudding took his finger into his mouth and came down with his fangs.

"*¡Chihuahua!*" Trucha roared as he shook his finger in pain. "You're a nasty *mocoso*."

"He's feisty, Trucha," Rudy said. "He bit my mom's finger too."

Trucha parked his bike in Rudy's backyard. The four boys and one cat marched off. Pudding was carried first by Rudy, then Alex, then Slinky, and finally Trucha. Each carried the cat, and each yelled from sharp bites that left little itchy punctures in their skin.

Rudy prayed that the woman—and the reward—would be home.

Rudy unfolded the wrinkled flyer again. He smoothed it out and read the address. Sure enough, this was it. The house was tall with weeds in the flower bed, and the grass shaggy and uncut. The porch light threw off a faint orange glow.

Pudding jumped from Trucha's arms and, tail flapping, raced to the front porch. A striped mother cat was asleep in the shade. Pudding whacked the sleeping cat, who jumped awake, startled. Pudding raised his back, a coil of terrorizing orneriness.

"You're bad," Trucha said as he climbed the front steps.

Pudding looked up at Trucha and hissed.

When Rudy knocked on the torn screen door, there was no answer. He knocked louder and longer, but still there was no answer. Rudy's heart knocked its two-beat clunk because Trucha was now glaring at him. Trucha was wetting his lips and pounding a fist into his palm.

"She's probably at the store," Rudy explained. He shrugged his shoulders and said lightly, "Let's wait on the lawn. Or if you want, I could go get you a soda, Trucha."

"Shut up, *sapo*," Trucha growled.

"She'll be here in a little bit," Rudy assured.

"Five minutes, *no más*," Trucha agreed. His shoulders were now square, ready to fight. "Then I got to take some kind of action."

"Trucha, it's my fault," Slinky whined.

"*Pues*, if it's your fault, then I take care of you first."

Slinky looked away, worried. His shoulders were rounded in fear. Rudy thought Slinky looked like a baby compared to Trucha, and like a baby, tears were welling up in his eyes.

"Can I go third, then?" Alex said.

"Yeah, man," Trucha sneered. "I'll save the best *nalga* whipping for last."

Rudy could see it coming. First Trucha would get them in headlocks and burn their scalps with knuckle burns. After that, he would pound the good air from their stomachs. Then he would jab them into a bloody mess. He gulped at this image and felt weak as he descended the porch.

The four started to fold their legs and sit on the lawn when a car drove up the driveway. A woman waved, tooted her car horn, and asked, "You the gardeners?"

Rudy rushed to the car and opened the door for the woman. She got out kicking sand from her sandals.

"I called you earlier. I found Pudding," Rudy announced.

"You did! Where is he?" she screamed happily. She ripped off her sunglasses and looked around.

"On the porch," Alex said, pointing.

But when their attention turned to the porch, Pudding wasn't there. Only the mother cat sat there, tall as a table lamp. Their gaze floated upward when they heard a meow. Pudding was on the roof, looking over the edge.

"You bad, bad cat," the woman scolded playfully. She clapped her hands and shouted, "Pudding, come down."

Pudding hissed and jabbed a paw at the woman.

"Where did you find him?" the woman asked Rudy.

"Near Belmont. Three days ago. I've been calling but there was no answer."

The woman explained that she had just got back from a vacation at Pismo Beach. She was happy to be home and happy for such a home-coming. She looked back at the roof, where Pudding was now washing himself.

"Ma'am," he asked, "is there still a reward? We need it pretty badly." He looked over at Trucha, whose face had gone soft. His shoulders were now relaxed.

"Of course. But who's going to get Pudding off the roof?"

"I'll do it," Alex volunteered.

"*Chale*, I'll do it," Slinky announced, wiping tears from the corners of his eyes. He turned to Trucha and said, with a bragging quaver in his throat, "See, I tol' you."

With Rudy's help, Slinky bellied his way onto the roof and brought down not only Pudding but a football lodged near the air-conditioning unit. He also brought down some more bites and scratches from Pudding, who hissed and meowed all the way to his mistress's outstretched arms.

Chapter 12

The reward was paid in crisp five-dollar bills, which Trucha snatched up with a greedy sneer on his face. Rudy and Alex thanked the woman and shook Pudding's paw, raza-style. They took off up the street chewing saltwater taffy, which the woman had brought from Pismo Beach.

Trucha was happy. He said that he was going to save the money to buy a moped.

"I'll be bad, homeboys," Trucha bragged. "I'll give you a ride when I'm not with my girl."

"Didn't you break up with Linda?" Alex asked. He was picking at his molars, where the taffy was stuck.

Slinky eyed Alex to be quiet, but it was too late. Big-mouth Alex had mentioned Linda Ruiz, Trucha's girlfriend—the one who had ridden sidesaddle on Slinky's bike with a rose between her teeth.

"*Simón*. Linda was okay, but now I got a *ruca* from Sequoia who's sweet on me."

"Let's go, Trucha," Slinky suggested. "Let's go to the playground, you and me, *carnal*, and jump in the pool."

Trucha snatched his bike from Rudy's backyard, and Slinky hopped onto the handlebars. They wobbled up the street, spitting sunflowers in the late summer air.

"Man, I'm glad that's over," Rudy sighed after they had left.

"*Órale*," Alex said. "Those dudes are scary."

They sat on Rudy's front porch. It was late afternoon, and the heat was flattening out to a simmer, not a boil.

"That was a pretty nice woman," Rudy said, referring to the owner of Pudding. "That *gatito* was bad, huh?"

"Yeah, he was a terror," Alex said. He looked at his arm, which was streaked with scratches. "If I were a dog, I'd be scared."

Rudy's mother called him from the front window. For a moment he thought she wanted him to mow the lawn or pull weeds. Or worse, clean up his room.

"*Mi'jo,*" she sang with a lilt in her voice. She poked her face from the window. She had a Walkman around her neck, the cables reaching far into her fluffy hair. "You have some mail, *mi'jo.*"

"Me?"

"Yeah!" she screamed. She was sweaty from doing aerobics in the living room. Her hair was tangled and her face flushed.

Rudy went inside to get his letter and asked his mother what was for dinner. Bouncing from foot to foot, she screamed over the music playing on her Walkman, "Chicken!"

Rudy took his letter outside, turning it over and over. "How come your mother is mad at you?" Alex asked. "What did you do?"

"She's not mad at me," answered Rudy.

"She called you chicken, didn't she?"

"Nah, homes. She said we're having chicken for dinner."

Rudy turned his attention to the letter. He held it skyward and saw a dollar bill smiling at him. Eyes big, he ripped open the envelope and snagged a wrinkled dollar.

"Who sent you that *feria*?" Alex inquired, totally confused. He wiggled a finger into the envelope, feeling for more. He squinted and peered in. *Nada.*

Right then, Rudy remembered the chain letters they had sent pleading for money to help the ozone and three boys in trouble.

"It's the letters we sent."

"What letters?"

"You know, homes. The ozone letters."

Alex's face brightened, and he sighed. "Oh, yeah, man. The ozone chain letters. My great idea!"

Rudy imagined other letters following in the coming days and all the bills he would stuff back into his limp money sock. He imagined buying his own Discman, which he would hang on his belt as he walked around the block. But the dream popped like a water balloon when his tongue ran across his dry lips.

"Let's go get a soda."

"With just one dollar?"

"I got some change." Rudy fumbled for a quarter in his pants pocket.

They headed to the store, free of worry. They bought sodas and looked at *Low Rider* magazine until the storekeeper told them to move on. They left the store with their empty soda cans. For the first block they wore the cans on their feet. The next block they stomped the cans flat on the sidewalk, remembering that each was worth five cents. They were working boys, and the future looked, after all, at least as bright as aluminum.

ABOUT THE AUTHOR

Born in Fresno, California, Gary Soto now lives in Berkeley. His books, including *Living Up the Street, A Summer Life, Small Faces,* and *The Skirt,* are often about growing up Mexican-American. He has also written fiction and poetry and has produced three short films for Spanish-speaking children.

His most recent book for Delacorte Press is *The Pool Party.*

ABOUT THE ILLUSTRATOR

Robert Casilla has illustrated many books for children. He lives in Yonkers, New York.